T0312429

BAD GRACES

Also by Kyrie McCauley

All the Dead Lie Down

KYRIE McCAULEY

BAD GRACES

Magpie Books
An imprint of HarperCollins*Publishers* Ltd
1 London Bridge Street
London SE1 9GF

www.harpercollins.co.uk

HarperCollins*Publishers*
Macken House,
39/40 Mayor Street Upper,
Dublin 1
D01 C9W8
Ireland

First published by HarperCollins*Publishers* Ltd 2024
1

A catalogue record for this book is available from the British Library.

ISBN: 978-0-00-861230-6 (HB)
ISBN: 978-0-00-861231-3 (TPB)

Typography by Molly Fehr

Printed and bound in the UK using 100% Renewable Electricity
by CPI Group (UK) Ltd

This book contains FSC™ certified paper and other controlled sources
to ensure responsible forest management.

For more information visit: www.harpercollins.co.uk/green

For quiet girls with feral hearts.
For loud girls with secret ones.

And for Adiah Wren,
who has the biggest heart of all.

If you don't look closely, you might think that the girl is asleep.

You would be wrong on two counts.

First, that she is asleep, and second, that she is a girl.

Her eyes are closed, and her cheeks are roses, wind-bitten but flushed with the promise of blood and life. If you don't lean in, you won't smell the sweet-sour death notes in the air around her, or notice that though the warmth hasn't quite left her face, the tips of her fingers are already a bright cerulean blue. They are the color of the morpho butterfly, or a clear spring sky, or a bluebird when the sun strikes his feathers just so. They are also the color of death.

The skin of her shoulders is too pale, her bloodlessness stark against the brilliant growth of dark green moss all around her. She is sprawled on a raised mound of pine needles and earth, and a trail of small indigo mushrooms circles her head, not unlike a crown.

From a distance, the soft dusting of blade-shaped scales above her ears could be mistaken for white-blond hair, and the protrusions from her back would stay hidden underneath the strange stillness of her body. Strange, if you think she's merely asleep. Not so strange if you know she's dead.

Stranger still are her wings, but they are folded and broken underneath her, undiscovered by your curious gaze.

She lies on the forest floor, body broken, a single drop of blood smeared on the edge of her lip. It is nearly dry now, its color darkened from the brilliant flash of fresh blood. The maroon looks like a bit of smudged lipstick forgotten from the night before.

The night before, when she had still been alive.

She had stretched those wings out, testing their weight as well as her own resolve. She'd climbed to the highest edge of cliff on their island, overlooking the sea. It was a view unmatched by any other her whole life—whether that life was a thousand years ago, or perhaps just one, it was hard for her to say. Time made less sense here.

She'd faced the vast, open ocean ahead of her, and she'd seen only the dark nothingness of the midnight sea. Endless miles of water, surrounding her completely all this time. Some days it had felt like a prison around her, and other days a refuge. But now it was time to go home. Time to launch her body off the cliff edge and let the air whip across these wings she'd once cursed but now prayed to.

Don't let me fall, she had asked the wind, her wish a silent echo repeating in her mind as she crept forward until her toes were exposed over the cliff. With only air beneath them, she felt a sharp tug at her navel from deep inside. Gravity was lying in wait like a leviathan in the water, ready to pull her down to the sharp rocks and inky darkness below.

It could have been sheer desperation that finally forced her feet from the edge just as dawn broke over the sea. The kind of desperation that comes when all other options have been exhausted.

But the truth is that it was love that made her take that final, terrible step over the edge. Love tempered by fires that few ever knew in their lifetime. Love that made her not only willing to take the risk, but eager to take it, simply for the hope of it all.

She fell so fast she barely remembered to stretch, stretch her wings, but she did remember, and she gasped when the wind caught beneath them.

She rose quickly after that, catching a warm thermal draft that lifted her up, away from the rocks, until she circled over the island, a small speck among the cotton-candy clouds. She closed her eyes and basked in the warmth of the sunrise on her face. She opened them again and found the early light of the morning reflecting off the softness of her wings, so thin the light shone through them, glowing pink.

Icarus flew, she thought.

In that moment, suspended above the island, she felt truly free. It was a potent sensation, more powerful than anything else she'd experienced. Ironic, to taste its sweetness so near to her death.

She was glorious, before the fall.

ACT I

The Kings Ship

For my part, the sea cannot drown me.

—*The Tempest*, Act III, Scene II

By the time I was twelve years old, I had lived in thirteen different homes.

There was something profound about that year for me. It was like standing on a precipice wishing I could jump already, even though I knew the fall might kill me.

Age twelve was my year of great epiphanies. One after another, like lightning chasing thunder, each of them changing the trajectory of my life in a way I didn't understand at the time. The first was the bittersweet realization that no one was coming to save me. Bitter to know that loneliness, and sweet to taste the freedom of no longer waiting on anyone else. If I wanted anything, I had to take it for myself. It was also the year that I learned my sister hated me more than anything in the world.

She was right to hate me. I was the troubled child, the rebellious one. I was the girl who set fire to House Seven. No, it was House Eight. The DeLucas.

We were there only a month before I found our foster dad's lighter and set the living room curtains ablaze. After that, we cycled quickly through Houses Nine through Twelve. A history of arson doesn't exactly boost a foster kid up the placement list, and I did absolutely nothing to reassure new parents willing to take me on. In House Ten, I cut off my own hair, shearing it as close to my scalp as I could, ignoring the hot flash of pain and blood when the scissors blade found flesh, leaving a thin line of a scar just at the hairline on my forehead.

I'd seen the notes in our shared file once. Our caseworker had been distracted, taking an emergency phone call, hoping to find us a new placement in time for the holidays. I'd just burned bridges at House Twelve by punching their biological son in the face. I still think I should have gotten credit for all the times I didn't punch him even though I wanted to. Some faces are just so very punch-worthy.

Everly was ignoring me, reading on the other side of the room. Everly was always reading. Foster parents loved that about her.

I grabbed our file as soon as we were alone and began to flip through it. *Everly is a good student, polite, quiet, well-mannered. She likes to draw and reads three grade levels up. She is kind and, though a bit shy, seems eager to make friends.*

Predictable. Boring. I turned the page.

Violet is temperamental, sometimes volatile, and occasionally violent with herself and others. Uninterested in making social connections. Liv has a diagnosed attention disorder and struggles in school. History of self-harm.

If anyone was trying to get to know me just from these pages, their outlook would be grim. My entire life was a series of incidents, laid out in black-ink bullet points by weary social workers. I scanned the rest of the pages. There was nothing on it I didn't already know about myself, but I realized my file was full of half-truths. No one knew why I cut my hair or punched my foster brother or set a house full of people on fire. Probably no one ever would know. People tended not to care about the why, and I didn't care to tell them.

At the bottom of the page was a space for recommendations. I'd been with the same caseworker for six or seven years by then, and I knew she hated me for what I'd put Everly through. Enough to recommend that if we didn't find a good placement for both of us soon, we should probably be separated.

And yet it wasn't until House Thirteen that I realized the depth of my sister's resentment. It was just a few days before our shared thirteenth birthday—a birthday that only our social worker acknowledged, with kids' meals from the local burger place and a few gently used "new" clothes from the donation bins.

I woke in the night to a pillow pressed to my face, held down with every bit of strength Everly had, though that wasn't much. We were both scrawny, scrappy little things, with long, ever-tangled hair and feral looks in our eyes. But Everly tried her damnedest that night. I was the problem. I was the instigator. The literal fire starter. A liability. I understood her logic perfectly. If she could just take me out of the equation, maybe she could find a family that would keep her for more than a few months.

The policy of Child Protective Services is to keep siblings together. I'm sure they thought we were a comfort to each other, a hand to hold as we shoved all our belongings into a black garbage bag to move from one foster placement to the next. But Everly had stopped reaching for my hand years ago. Her anger had built steadily and quietly, until she couldn't bear it anymore. Until she tried to kill me, just so I would stop ruining her life.

That night I scratched at her until her arms and hands were slick with blood. It was fortunate for me that no one really cared about our basic hygiene at that point and my nails had grown out, long and sharp. I was like a rabid creature, clawing at her until she let go of the pillow on my face. I left deep gouges from her elbows to the backs of her hands.

Everly collapsed onto the bed beside me, sobbing.

"I hate you," she whispered between hiccups as I wrapped my arms around her.

"I know. I know you do. It's okay. I forgive you. I understand."

I continued to murmur low words of comfort until she fell asleep. In that moment, I understood her better than I ever had before. Finally, she was angry the way I was angry. Finally, she fought to survive, instead of living quietly in my shadow, always a step behind me. It was the first time I saw her as her own unique self. Before that, she'd felt like an extension of me. When she hurt, I hurt, like a skinned knee, raw and stinging in all the places I was exposed. But she wasn't a person I loved, and I wasn't someone she loved. We were more like strange appendages of each other. Or tumors, nestled deep in each other's guts and heads.

Undetectable until it made us sick.

After that night, I stopped setting fires, both literal and figurative. We still flew through the next three houses in quick succession—this time for reasons besides me—and then we met the Millers.

Rachel and Toby had been married for two decades and had decided early on that they didn't want children. It wasn't until they neared their fifties that they changed their minds. They had their dream careers, a beautiful house in San Diego, and a neat retirement plan on the horizon, but by some strange twist of fate, they also wanted us.

They loved Everly instantly. They tolerated me. And at first, that was enough. I'd learned to adapt to a thousand changes before, and this last one was easy once I accepted it.

Still, I never felt lonely before the Millers.

They didn't mean to exclude me. I'd built the walls all myself; I couldn't be upset that no one was willing to do the hard work of climbing them to be close to me. Especially with Everly standing right out in the open, ready for love.

I tell myself that that's why I decide to leave. To let Everly have the family she always dreamed of for herself. I'd hardly be the first foster runaway. No one would miss me, Everly least of all. We'd eventually reached a kind of tentative balance in our relationship, something more like endurance than warmth.

But it is Everly who leads me to my way out. It's no more than a coincidence, really. Or luck, for perhaps the first time in my life. She leaves the paperwork right in the center of the dining table. An invitation to apply, one among dozens that Everly receives for some prestigious opportunity or another. She wouldn't have glanced at this one twice—it is a writing contest, and Everly prefers math and science. She wants to be an environmentalist one day. She doesn't notice when I slip it off the table and into my backpack.

Volatile and occasionally violent, uninterested in making social connections.

I'd never understood the phrase *lone wolf*—even wolves have packs. Instead, I think of a bear. Solitary. Volatile. Occasionally violent. That was me. Never meant to be part of a family. But singularly capable of surviving even the harshest of winters.

In my eagerness to open it, I drag the edge of the envelope along my skin, slicing a neat line across my fingertip that wells blood immediately.

I ignore the sting, as well as the droplet of crimson that lands on the letter as I unfold it, smeared right across the embossed golden seal, soaking into the cream-colored paper.

Dear Ms. Whitlock, We are pleased to inform you . . .

The letter is from the Shakespeare Center, offering a summer internship on the set of a movie filming in Alaska, starting in two weeks. It's the prize for the winning application, out of the thousands submitted by young writers across the country.

For several minutes, I just stand there, holding it carefully in my hands, sucking on my finger. Then I fold the blood-stained page and put it neatly back in its envelope.

I hide it underneath my pillow.

Then I cross to the hall bathroom and yank at the toilet

paper, wrapping it around my finger. Paper cuts have no right to hurt as much as they do.

"Gross," says a voice in the doorway. Everly is there with her nose wrinkled at me in disgust. "You're practically begging for an infection," she adds. "Come here."

I follow her into her room and fall onto the bed with the least amount of grace possible. Her room is neat. She has a place for everything, and posters of national parks pinned on the walls. A canvas banner hangs over her bed, displaying perfect rows of her enamel pin collection. There is one on the edge with a picture of the Loch Ness monster that says: *The important thing is that I believe in myself.*

I wrinkle my nose in distaste.

Everly has become one of those perpetually positive people. The ones who say things like *Everything happens for a reason,* or *Just stay positive,* or the worst: *If I can do it, so can you.* At first it was annoying, but now it's downright toxic. It's like she's erased all the bad memories from her head. It's like she's left them all to me.

Everly fishes out a first aid pack—probably one of many—from somewhere and is already putting antibiotic cream on a small bandage. She takes a pair of cuticle scissors and cuts the sticky ends of the bandage, wrapping them around my finger crisscross so it stays in place. All her movements are meticulous and practiced.

I'm too impatient for this. For her.

"Just put it on, Everly. This isn't surgery."

"Your recklessness will be your downfall," Everly says.

"And your perfectionism will be yours," I snap right back.

When Everly finishes her ministrations, she doesn't so much drop my hand as toss it away from her. I guess the brief truce formed by my bleeding finger has ended.

In our last three years with the Millers, Everly has bloomed. She is quite a bit taller than me now, and her hair is long, shining and yellow. A literal golden child. She loves all the same things Rachel loves: hiking and volunteering with rescue animals and collecting tiny ridiculous things like spoons and pins. They spend Friday nights together watching baking shows.

Tobias Miller is aloof but kind. He seems to think the extent of fatherhood is cracking the occasional bad pun and making sure we are provided for, an arrangement that suits me just fine. Things with the Millers are safe, at least, if not comfortable. But I knew that the letter under my pillow could change everything.

"What are you doing now that our classes are done?" I ask, a deliberate and likely transparent attempt to bridge the uncomfortable silence stretching between us.

"Volunteering at the shelter a few days a week," she says. "And a bunch of us are going camping next week . . . if you want to come."

Everly likes to go camping with her friends in the summer,

almost every weekend. At first, I thought they did it as an excuse to party out in the woods, but when I joined her once I realized I was wrong. Her friends were like her, good and smart. They liked building fires and lying out under the stars and talking about their ambitious plans. It was a conversation I had very little to contribute to. Unlike Everly, I was still in survival mode from our childhood. I couldn't think that far ahead. It felt like tempting fate to even pretend I had a future.

"And be a walking mosquito feast? No, thank you." I doubt the invitation was genuine anyway. Her friends couldn't stand me, and I thought they were boring. "You do know that we can sleep in houses and take hot showers, right? You don't have to go torture yourself in the wilderness every weekend."

"It isn't torture," Everly says. "You might be surprised, Liv, if you just—"

"I'll leave the hiking to you." I interrupt her before she can finish her sentence with my most hated word: *try*. Everyone always tells me I'm not trying hard enough. But I do try, and the only conclusion I can draw is that it's me. I am not enough. "Let me know when you take up glamping."

I use Everly's least-favorite made-up word on purpose, and it has the desired effect: she rolls her eyes and turns away, dismissing me.

At the door, I thank her for the bandage. The gesture was kind, and our relationship is fragile at best, weakened by years of animosity. But she is already ignoring me, her nose, as usual, in a book: *The Forager's Guide to Mushrooms*.

That's Everly's idea of reading for fun.

My own room is the exact inverse of my sister's. My bed is unmade, and there are books and notebooks sprawled across it. My desk is a museum of my abandoned projects—a watercolor set, paintbrushes dried to the plastic lid; a stack of photographs I was halfway through hanging on the line of twine I have strung across my wall; my last trigonometry assignment for the summer class that I gave up on days ago. I'm going to pass the makeup class, and that is good enough. By the end of next year, I should be on track to graduate, despite falling behind during all our moves.

If Everly is the academic, then I'm the artist. I'd cycled through all the mediums—photography, painting, a summer spent toying with Toby's old acoustic guitar. I'd landed on poetry last year, and I fell hard for it, flying through the tattered copies on Rachel's shelves. It was the first time I entered the school library willingly, and their paltry poetry section lasted me two weeks. Plath, Angelou, Oliver, Rich. Emily Dickinson and Edna St. Vincent Millay. I'd never found myself in the pages of a book before I found those women and their secret, hidden inner selves. So much of it was raw, bright red and pulsing like a fresh burn on skin.

Finally, I'd found something to match my own teeming insides.

Not that it made me a better student. If anything, I was more distracted than ever, writing instead of listening in class, slipping ever further behind until summer classes were mandated.

I reach for the laptop that Rachel and Toby gave me for Christmas, an incentive to catch up in school and graduate with Everly. I think it was meant to be nice, but it felt like a ticking clock on how long I would be welcome in their home.

A quick online search brings up the Shakespeare Center's website. I scroll through their education programs until I find the essay-writing contest and its grand prize, a six-week internship on the set of a film production—an adaptation of Shakespeare's *The Tempest,* filming in Alaska over the summer.

When I search the film's title, a recent press release pops up, dated a few days ago. The image that loads is a paparazzi photo of Paris Grace, with her wide white smile and sleek long hair dyed bright Barbie pink.

She is perhaps the most famous singer on the planet, and she is barely seventeen. She'd released a new album a few months ago and, according to the article, was completing her world tour just in time to join the production in Alaska, her first bold move away from music and into the film industry. The author of the article thought this was a mistake. *Paris Grace should stick to what she knows.*

The only other names listed in the article are Vincent Bellegarde, former heartthrob turned producer who now poured his money into pet projects like this one, and finally, the Knight sisters. The British girls are actresses, and they skyrocketed to fame when they both earned Oscar nominations the same year for their roles in *Little Women*. I cried watching Miri Knight's portrayal of Beth March, and I never cry over movies.

I lock my bedroom door before pulling the envelope out from under my pillow. I run my hand over the name addressed on the front with a kind of reverence that I've never really felt before. It is the opportunity of a lifetime for someone like me. Someone with a troubled past and mediocre grades and *underdeveloped social skills*, according to the school guidance counselor.

One time I'd gotten up the nerve to take my writing to that same guidance counselor. I needed to know how people pursued careers in the arts. Especially people who came from nothing, like me. She'd taken the file from me—inside I'd tucked a dozen poems, sonnets, and stories. She'd read it all, silently, in front of me. Then she peered at me over her glasses. "Did you take these from someone else?"

"No," I told her. I wasn't even offended by the question. If she thought I'd stolen them, then she thought they were good.

She looked back down at the pages, thumbing through them, reading them again. She sighed and said the next bit somewhat to herself, almost under her breath, but not quite.

"It won't be enough."

I'd grabbed the folder and stormed out. My school file might as well have had large block letters stamped across it that said *LOST CAUSE*.

After that, I stopped writing entirely, until I found out about this contest.

Before I can overthink it, I call the number listed on the letter and tell them I would love to accept the internship. I write down the travel details—I would need to be in Los Angeles for departure in exactly ten days to catch the private chartered flight to Alaska, and I quickly accept their offer to book a hotel room for me the night before. They tell me how to log in to complete the necessary paperwork.

After I hang up, I go online and buy a bus ticket, the cheapest I can find so it won't raise any flags with Rachel. No one would notice until long after I was gone. Then I log in to the foundation's website and fill out the forms. There is a section where your parents have to sign for permission and the liability waivers, but it's as simple as typing in Rachel's name. I change one digit of her cell phone number so they can't actually reach her if they try to call. At least not right away.

Ten days and I would be out of here, and I didn't plan on ever coming back. The internship was a means to an end—a place to go, connections to make, new cities to explore. The five-grand cash prize for the winner is my golden ticket to start a new life. My own life.

When it gets late enough that I'm sure everyone is asleep, I sneak into the backyard to the firepit that Toby built two summers ago, and I light a small fire in the bottom. When the flames grow hot, little sparks leap up at me, and I pull the letter out of my pocket and drop it in.

It burns fast, edges curling inward and blackening. I stay until it turns to ash. Until there is no evidence that it existed.

Erasing the fact that it was never addressed to me at all.

Exactly ten days later I arrive at a boat dock instead of an airport. There was a last-minute change in our travel plans, all at the whim of Hollywood legend Vincent Bellegarde.

I wasn't even told of the change until I was checking out of my hotel room to head to my flight and the front desk gave me the message, nothing more than an address to give my driver. Now that I am standing on the dock under the predawn sky, watching as the taillights of my rideshare turn the corner, I realize I don't have nearly enough information. There are at least a dozen yachts docked on the pier, and not a soul around.

I toss my faded purple backpack on the ground and sit on my suitcase. Or rather, I sit on Rachel's suitcase that I'd swiped from the attic yesterday morning before walking to the bus stop.

While I wait for signs of life, I pick at my ruined cuticles and imagine a scenario where this entire internship was some twisted prank, and I'd have to go back to my foster parents and the sister whose identity I'd tried to steal.

Then there is a soft squeal of tires behind me, and I turn and watch a limousine pull up. The driver hops out and quickly whips around the vehicle to open the door before moving to the trunk to unload the luggage.

Paris Grace steps out of the limousine. Her hair is bubblegum pink now, not the bright fuchsia it had been in the press release photo. Her entire outfit is coordinated in pastels that match her hair—lavender and buttercup yellow and a soft shade of sage green. Even her purse is light pink, shaped like a heart and too small to hold anything useful.

There is a surreal moment where Paris simply stares at me, and I stare back. It is so absurd that I could be here, with her, about to board a luxury yacht to go to a film set.

Paris moves first, approaching me, her heels smacking against the wood.

"You must be the contest winner," she says.

I expect condescension in her tone, my defensiveness already starting to kick in, when I realize that there wasn't any malice in her words. She was stating a fact. There is only one reason a girl like me would be in a place like this: charity.

"Sorry, what's your name again? Avery? Emily?"

"Oh, I just go by Liv. Liv Whitlock."

Liv had been my nickname since I was six. One of our

early foster mothers had three Violets placed with her that year alone, and she couldn't keep us straight, so I became Liv. At first, I hated it. I felt like a stray dog being handed a new name on a collar. But the nickname stuck with me through the next three foster homes, somehow finding its way into my official file, and eventually it grew on me. Liv. *Live*. It was what I planned to do. I planned to survive.

"*Liv*," she says, testing my name in her mouth. "That's cute. I'm Paris."

I can't help but laugh. Yes, I know. Obviously, I know.

"It's nice to meet you," I say instead, refusing to be starstruck by a girl my age.

"I read your work," Paris says, surprising me for the second time in twenty seconds. "My agent reps the director over at the Shakespeare Center, so he sent your application to me. Thought I might like to know a little about you before we traveled together."

She's read the application. The one in which every answer to every question was about Everly, not me. Everly's grade point average, her school attendance, her extracurricular activities. Even her name. The only thing genuinely mine was the writing itself. I knew that as Violet, I didn't stand a chance. Talent could carry me so far, and then my reputation would follow like a freight train in its wake, destroying every delicate thing I'd built.

But as Everly? Everly Whitlock shone on paper. Volatile,

occasionally violent Violet did not. And now Paris Grace knew things that could tangle up my lies if she cared to dig into the details of that application.

"Why *are* we traveling together?" I ask, gently changing the subject.

I don't know what I had been expecting when the concierge at the hotel told me there'd been a change. At half past four I was still blinking away the lingering remnants of my dreams when we'd had the brief conversation, and it wasn't as though he knew, either.

But I wasn't expecting this—a private yacht, with Paris Grace herself as my companion.

Paris only shrugs.

"It was all Vincent's idea. He's impulsive like that. C'mon, let's at least get on board and then we can yell at him for causing so much confusion."

Paris doesn't wait for my agreement. She lifts her hand to beckon her driver, who begins to bring her things down to the dock.

"Do you know which boat?" I hike my backpack onto my shoulder and reach for my suitcase.

Paris talks to me without turning around.

"No, but I know Vincent Bellegarde. And he always has the biggest yacht on the dock."

Right. *Yacht,* not boat.

Paris leads the way, climbing right up the dock of a large

white ship with the name *Bianca* painted in script on its side.

"This must be it," Paris says. "He always names them after his ex-wives."

"Charming," I say, rolling my small suitcase up the bridge behind me.

"That's just Vincent," she says. "I've been to dozens of his parties. He takes some getting used to, but he's mostly harmless."

The word *mostly* is doing some heavy work in that sentence. I wish she'd just say it outright, but that isn't how it's done. When girls point fingers, we're called hysterical, or liars. So instead, we whisper soft warnings to each other, and we learn to listen for them in turn. A kind of trial by fire with our young bodies on the line.

So, when Paris says *mostly*, I tuck the word away inside, stuck somewhere between my ribs where it is just uncomfortable enough that I won't forget about it. That I won't let my guard down on this trip. No one ever actually tells you that navigating girlhood is like walking a minefield. One wrong step could kill you. I guess they expect you to learn that on your own.

And we do.

Then he was there, as though Paris had manifested him with her words, or maybe I had with my thoughts.

"Good morning, ladies." Vincent Bellegarde steps out of the cockpit in aviator sunglasses and a baseball cap. His casual address and appearance make him seem supremely human and approachable, unlike Paris, who acts and looks the part of celebrity in her heart-shaped sunglasses, tapping her foot impatiently against the sleek, planked floor of the yacht.

Vincent climbs down to the lower deck. He extends his hand, and we take turns shaking it. "I hope you don't mind the change of plans," he says with just a hint of a Southern drawl. "We've got some time before filming starts and I thought, well, why the hell don't we make the most of it and get to know each other."

"Sure, Vincent. This isn't just an excuse to write off your yacht expenses as part of the film?"

"Two birds, Ms. Grace. Two birds."

Some others have started arriving, and for a while it's a chaotic exchange of chauffeurs and personal assistants and luggage into rooms before we all gather back on the deck. Vincent emerges on the upper deck and addresses us from there like a king on his throne.

"All right." Vincent claps his hands together. "Introductions. I'm Vincent, this is my ship. I'll be navigating us up the coast of sunny California into Canada and then on to Alaska, with the assistance of Captain Wilson." Vincent turns to look behind him and calls out. "Wave to the nice ladies, Wilson!"

A man leans out of the cockpit and gives us a brief wave. He is older, maybe in his sixties, with salt-and-pepper hair and a matching, neatly trimmed beard. I'm more relieved than I'd care to admit that we won't be on the open ocean with only a movie star navigating.

There are a few additional crew members on board whom Vincent introduces. There is a chief officer, which Vincent explains is the same as a first mate, there to manage the cargo and crew and assist the captain with the ship as needed. The young man is introduced simply as Jacob, and we learn that he is actually the captain's son, eagerly following in his father's footsteps. Last is a middle-aged woman named Ms. Simmons, introduced as a professional chef and the ship steward.

Vincent drones on, and eventually I stop listening. He's spouting off a list of his accolades as though everyone here doesn't know who he is. I take the opportunity to study the others who have come on board.

I'm surrounded by girls, all around my own age. The notable difference between me and them is that they almost all have familiar, quite famous faces. Effie and Miri Knight, the British actress sisters, are standing to my right.

Effie is the elder of the two—nearly eighteen now, I think—and she's tall, probably just shy of six feet. She has brilliant natural red hair that is twisted up into a neat bun on the top of her head, leaving her shoulders exposed. Her skin is white and bathed in freckles, all over her aquiline nose and pointed face and down across those graceful bare shoulders. Effie Knight is the reason girls are tattooing freckles onto their own bodies. Effie is not so much pretty as she is striking. She has the kind of sharp features that will be interesting whether she's eighteen or eighty.

Miri Knight's hair is paler than sunshine, so fair that it's nearly white. She wears it half pulled up in a messy knot with the rest falling in soft waves down to her narrow shoulders. She is shorter than her sister, with a rounder face and none of Effie's freckles, and a little button nose just slightly upturned. Despite her small stature and soft features, she has a presence that seems to demand attention. She stands so sure of herself, her place here, her craft. Miri Knight is sixteen years old and already hitting the height of her career.

And I think she knows it.

On my left is Rosalind Torres. Last summer, Rosa dominated at the Olympics, bringing home a pile of gold gymnastics medals. She is Puerto Rican, with light brown skin and the biggest brown eyes I've ever seen. She's even shorter than Miri, and more petite, but strong. She's the only girl in the group besides me who carried her own luggage on board, even though the large duffel bag was nearly as tall as her. I watched her on television last year. She flipped so fast across her floor routine that I couldn't keep my eyes on her. It was like she could teleport. I'd heard she might be retiring from the sport, but that couldn't be true. She was poised to stand in the Olympic spotlight for years to come.

"We've got plenty of time, so we won't be hurrying," Vincent says, and I return my attention to the upper deck again, hopeful that he's wrapping up his monologue. "We've even got a few special detours planned. So welcome aboard, my ship is your ship, make yourselves at home. Trust that you are in good, good hands."

"More like grabby, grabby hands," Rosa mutters under her breath beside me, so soft I don't think any of the others heard until Paris gently smacks Rosa's arm to shush her.

That's red flag number two.

"Whatever, it's just a few days, and he'll be busy with his little toy," Paris says quietly, gesturing to the yacht, though the comment earns a sharp look from Effie Knight.

"Happy sailing, Vincent. Try not to get us killed," Paris calls out.

Vincent waves off the comment, lighting a cigar before disappearing into the cockpit. I guess that means we are dismissed.

The Knight sisters have stepped away from the group, and they are whispering in low, tense tones. Miri is waving wildly toward the cockpit, but Effie only crosses her arms. Finally, Miri throws her arms up in surrender, and Effie climbs the stairs and goes into the cockpit, too.

Miri rejoins us, quietly fuming.

Across from me is the last girl in the group. She is taller than me, but not by much. Her skin is dark brown, and she wears her black hair in long braids that frame either side of her face. She has high, round cheekbones. She's wearing a flowy sundress that is as bright blue as the California summer sky above.

She's the only face I don't recognize from magazine covers and movie posters.

"Thank god, another normal human being," she says in a lilting British accent, stepping forward to take my hand and squeeze it gently. "Celia Jones. I'm an old friend of Miri's, from, like, before she got all stupid famous or whatever."

"Now, now," Paris says, stepping over to wrap her arm around Celia's waist, "Celia has her own kind of fame, don't you?"

"Do you?" I ask.

"No, I don't," Celia insists. "I just have some popular social media channels, that's all."

"She has millions of followers," Paris explains. "And she uses it to encourage little girls to pursue STEM careers."

"Celia is a bit of a genius, though she'll never admit it," Miri says next to me. They're the first words she's spoken out loud, and I'm surprised by her speaking voice. She must notch it up to a slightly higher pitch when she's acting, because her real voice is much lower in person, rather deep for her small stature. Husky and warm.

When I look up, her eyes find mine, and they are quite large for her face, giving her an almost startled, doe-like appearance. But her sustained eye contact makes me feel like I'm the deer caught in headlights in front of her. Her eyes are green, but in the way the sea around us is green, because they're also a little yellow, and a little blue, reflecting all the light of the sun back again.

"I think you mean Celia is an influencer," Paris says with a laugh, and Celia reaches for her, wrapping her arms around her and trying to cover her mouth.

"You *swore* you wouldn't call me that," Celia says, but she's laughing, too. Paris pulls Celia's hand away and pacifies her teasing with a kiss.

Celia blushes and pulls back, putting a few inches between her and Paris.

"Oh, wait." I put it all together. "You two were together on the cover of—"

"Don't say it," Celia says, holding up her hand. "That rat-bastard tabloid is trying to ruin our lives."

"Sorry," I offer, embarrassed at my misstep. "I swear I didn't even read it. I only saw the cover at the grocery store."

It feels a little gross that I know so much about these girls, but only the things that were deemed worthy of clickbait headlines and gossip websites. I probably know as few truths about them as they know about me.

"It's all right. Celia's just . . . very private," Paris says. If she's bothered by Celia pulling away, she doesn't show it. "They weren't wrong about us. We just don't think our relationship is anyone's business but ours."

"You're right," I say. "It's not."

"Thanks," Paris says. "Hey, everyone meet Liv. She won that Shakespeare contest and is now doomed to spend her summer with us in the middle of nowhere, Alaska."

"Really?" Miri asks, a minor frown forming across her face. "It was your application?"

"Don't tell me you read it, too?" I ask.

But Miri's confusion clears, and she inclines her head as though she's appraising me anew.

"We're glad to have you," she says. "Someone with some real-life perspective to keep us grounded."

There was a shuddering movement beneath our feet. The yacht began to move away from the dock, its motions smooth.

"And we're off," Paris says. "I'm going to get high. Any of you are welcome to join me."

"She gets horribly seasick, and it helps," Celia says to me.

"Remember the Amalfi Coast last Christmas?" Rosa asks. "She couldn't even leave her bed."

I realize then that all these girls have known each other for some time. They've traveled together. They're friends, the five of them. More than ever, I know I don't belong here.

Paris covertly slips her hand into Celia's, tugging her along to the stairs that lead down to the living quarters. I'd only caught a glimpse inside the yacht when I took my bags down, but everything looked elegant and expensive. Details that spoke of luxury I'd only seen in movies before today.

Rosa and Miri follow, and at the top of the stairs Miri turns back, waiting for me.

She gives me the barest hint of a smile. I get the sense that Miri Knight is studying me like I'm some strange specimen that she's trying to understand.

I know that look. I've seen it my whole life. I'm out of place here, and she doesn't even know I cheated my way to get here.

"Are you coming, Liv?" she asks.

"In a few minutes," I say. "Thanks."

They go inside, and I walk to the railing of the broad deck, trying to shake the feeling that has settled in my gut that something is wrong. I haven't felt this way since our first nights in new houses, when I would pull blankets tight over my entire body, head and all, like a cocoon. I would hide away from the dark, from the strangeness of unfamiliar noises and smells. The darkness under my blanket always felt different from the dark outside of it, I think because it was mine. If I created the darkness by pulling the blanket over my head, that meant I controlled it. And if I was in control, then I didn't have to be afraid.

I'd learned from such a young age to trust my instincts, and all my internal alarm bells are ringing now: a sour stomachache and a racing heart. Maybe I'm seasick, like Paris. *Or maybe it's because you're a liar,* a little voice in my head sneers at me. *You don't deserve this.*

It isn't even my own voice—that honor belongs to my sister.

I stay on the deck until the shoreline shrinks, until all I see is green, and then nothing. In art class last year our assignment was to create a self-portrait, but as an object. I painted blue and gray ocean waves, crashing up against the rocky coast of an island. Then I covered the green trees onshore in a dense fog like a shroud. Like a shield. Like a scratchy blanket in a strange home.

I once read somewhere that no man is an island.

But I think maybe girls are.

Vincent Bellegarde has the kind of charm that makes you forget yourself. His voice is honey-sweet, and he calls all us girls *darling* and *ma'am*. A Southern gentleman through and through, until he isn't.

Vincent had been in the cockpit with Captain Wilson most of the day, venturing into the living quarters only for meals. He had a habit of popping champagne over every meal, casually serving us underage.

"I fold," Vincent says from across the table that night. Right when we finished dinner, Vincent pulled out a deck of cards to teach the six of us how to play poker. He didn't bother to ask if we already knew how to play, and we've managed to beat him almost every game.

"Too bad we aren't playing for clothes. Did I ever tell you about the time I played against the entire cast of—"

"Yes, Vincent," Paris cuts him off. "You have. And we aren't stripping."

Vincent throws his hands up defensively.

"I wouldn't dare suggest it," he says, and laughs. He puffs on his cigar and glances down at his watch. "Wilson says we are progressing beautifully. Perfect weather. We're pulling away from the coast now; it's our best chance of seeing whales."

"Is that safe?" I ask. I've been sipping champagne, and between the alcohol and the rocking of the boat, I'm feeling light-headed, so I set the glass away from me. I've never liked drinking. That sensation of being detached from your body. It makes me feel vulnerable. Vincent Bellegarde makes me feel vulnerable, too.

"Of course it's safe, sweetheart. What kind of chaperone would I be if I led you lovely young ladies into danger? Besides, I promised grand detours, and Vincent Bellegarde is a man of his word."

I'm sure he means for his wink to reassure me, but it does the exact opposite.

"Would you like to play one last round?" Paris asks, twisting her pink hair around her finger and fixing Vincent with her amber-brown eyes. Her pile of winnings sits in front of her. She'd won most of the games, and if we'd been playing for real money, she'd be up a few grand.

"I'll pass, darlin'. I ought to head up to the deck and give old Wilson a break. He needs his beauty sleep, too."

Vincent rises from his seat but doesn't leave. He hovers

there, as though he's waiting for something. His gaze lands on Effie, still sitting at his elbow.

"Effie, love. Won't you join me for a little while? I'll get so lonely up there on my own." The tone of his voice has changed, just slightly, and now it's too sweet, too honeyed, nearly cloying as his hand drifts to her shoulder and his fingers squeeze. On Effie's skin, I can see the imprint of each finger when he lifts it away.

"Of course," Effie says, getting up and following him.

The yacht shifts unsteadily and Vincent stumbles on his way to the stairs. Effie moves quickly so that she is right beside him, her arm wrapped around him as she guides him out. She is murmuring softly to him, but I can't make out any of the words.

Miri rolls her eyes at her sister and cleans up the cards, but Paris is turned to the stairs, watching until they disappear above deck, scowling at them.

"He's kind of the worst," Paris says. She moves to the sofa, curling up beside Celia and pulling her hands into her lap. Celia looks unsure, and I get the sense that they aren't usually so open about their relationship.

"He always has been," Rosa mumbles in agreement, slinking off the chair and stretching her body out across the plush carpet floor. She twists into a split, bending forward until her face is pressed flat, her arms extended out in front of her. "Why do you guys tolerate him again?"

"Because Effie says we have to." Miri stands up so fast she knocks her chair over. She leaves it on the ground, rounding the table and pulling open the massive refrigerator. She stands there a moment as though she's considering its contents, and then slams the door shut. "And because he's single-handedly funding this project."

I pick up Miri's chair and slide it under the table.

"Do you even want to do Shakespeare?" Celia asks. She seems to have relaxed now that Vincent has gone. She leans her head on Paris's shoulder.

"It's better than the other projects the studio kept handing us." Miri turns around and pulls herself up onto the counter of the kitchen island, crossing her legs beneath her.

"Are you absolutely sure you don't want to be a princess?" Rosa asks from the floor with a laugh, her voice muffled. "I still can't believe you turned down the house of the mouse. You'd make a perfect Rapunzel."

"I can't do it," Miri says. "I'll be trapped with that image forever if I do. I've been cast as the ingénue too many times already. They see my big round eyes and they think, *Great, Bambi,* and then stick me in these delicate, sappy little roles. No, thank you."

"But you were a perfect Beth," I say.

Everyone turns to look at me. I think they'd forgotten I was even there.

"Thank you . . . Liv, was it?" Miri asks, and I nod, my

face heating under her scrutiny. "I just don't want to play the same role forever."

"Miri's already achieved perfection," Celia says. "Where *does* one go from there?"

"Well, when you reach your peak at sixteen, I'm afraid the only way to go is down." Miri laughs as she says it, giving herself a thumbs-down for emphasis, but there is something biting in the words, some deep truth to them, and I think everyone hears it.

A strained silence fills the room, and I can't help but feel like I was the cause. Miri's dark look seems to support my theory.

"Well, I'm exhausted," I say. "I'm going to get some sleep."

"But the night is young!" Rosa shouts from the side of the room. She is upside down in a perfect handstand, and slowly keels over into an arch before standing. Her face is flushed, and little curls frame her face. "We're breaking into Vincent's good whiskey later."

"Leave her alone, Rosa," Celia says. "We've got weeks to scare Liv properly; let's not spoil it all on the first night, right? Besides, I'm wiped. We're crashing soon, too."

I give an awkward wave and slip away down the hall before anyone else can protest, grateful to Celia for giving me an out. It isn't that they aren't nice. But I've got nothing in common with them, and it feels like every conversation leads back to how out of place I am here.

My room is small, but every detail points to luxury. There are crystal glasses on the bar, locked into place beside a complimentary bottle of Dom Pérignon.

I'm pleased to find that the lights in my room can be dimmed, and I stand in the doorway playing with the light switch, running the lights as bright as they go and then back down again. I don't turn them all the way off, opting to leave a glow in the room.

Sixteen years old, and I still hate the dark. It's mortifying, but I can't help it. In the dark, I'm a little kid again, in an unknown place, with people who are strangers.

The sheets are the softest I've ever climbed into, and despite the newness of . . . well, everything, I am quickly lulled to sleep by the rocking of the ship on gentle waves and the warmth of the alcohol in my bloodstream. It feels like only seconds pass before I'm woken by someone calling my name from my doorway.

"Liv. *Liv!*" the voice whispers furiously. "Hurry up!"

I sit up fast, and my fuzzy brain tries to convince me I'm back with the Millers, or the DeLucas, or the Andersons, and that the voice must belong to Everly.

The jostling boat reminds me where I am.

It's Miri at the door. Her navy crewneck sweatshirt ends mid-thigh, and if she's wearing shorts underneath, I can't see them. She's giggling and trying to contain the noise by putting her own hand over her mouth. The gesture does little to contain the hearty peal of laughter, but it is so genuine and weirdly endearing, and I laugh, too.

"Come see this! Quick!" With that, she's gone from the doorway, and a moment later I hear her stumbling up the stairs that lead to the deck.

She's going to get herself killed, stumbling around up there drunk.

I hurry out of bed, throwing my shoulder-length hair into a messy knot so it's out of my face. The hallway and living area are dimly lit by running lights along the floor and under the cabinets of the small galley, and I'm able to make it to the stairs.

Up on the deck, I suck in a deep breath of sea air, so cold it hurts my chest.

I should have grabbed a sweatshirt.

Miri is ahead of me on the deck, arms draped over the railing, her grip too loose and too casual for the fact that certain death awaits if she falls overboard in the night with no one looking.

She turns back and waves me forward.

"Look!" she says as I join her at the railing. "Watch, just there."

The moon is bright and high and full, painting the dark sea with streaks of light.

I watch where she's pointing. I stand there so long I wonder if this is some kind of weird prank or initiation, or maybe she's lured me up here to shove me off the ship that I lied my way onto. When I shiver, Miri's arm goes around me without a word. The hem of her sweatshirt lifts to reveal that she is wearing only underwear beneath, no pajamas. Her bare leg presses against me and I can feel how warm she is despite her lack of clothes.

I look back to her face, embarrassed to have even noticed what she's wearing. But Miri isn't concerned. Her green-gray eyes are bright and clear, not clouded with alcohol like I'd expected, and they're trained on the water.

"There! There it is!" She points out at the waves as a massive shadow rises on the horizon, directly in front of us.

Not a shadow, but rather a whale as it breaches the water.

It is so incredibly huge that I stand in actual slack-jawed awe at the sight of it. When the whale crashes back into the ocean, a thousand droplets of water rise in its wake, carrying moonlight on them like falling stars.

"Isn't that amazing?" Miri asks, turning to face me.

"It's the most incredible thing I've ever seen," I tell her, and I mean it.

We wait for a few minutes longer, and we're rewarded when the whale jumps again, this time even closer, the side of its body rising like a wide gray wall in the ocean.

The whale rises once more, this time only surfacing for air instead of breaching the waves, but it does so just beyond the stern of the ship. Miri and I are showered with ocean water. Miri starts to laugh, holding up her hands as it rains down on us.

"Oi, thanks for that, gorgeous!" she yells at the sea.

We stay there for a while longer without discussing it, our eyes hopeful on the ocean for another sighting. My arms are still bare, though, and I start to shiver.

"Hey, it's freezing out here," Miri says. "Let's head back down."

I wish we could stay out here all night, just in case the whale returns, but now that the giddiness has worn off, I feel the full chill of the air.

"Yeah, okay," I agree, rubbing my hands up and down my arms, in part to warm them, but also to cover my scars before Miri notices them. Ugly marks from an ugly past. Memories I don't want to bring into this new world I've found.

When we reach the door that leads into the living area, I notice Captain Wilson standing on the deck above us.

At first, I think he was watching for the whales, too, but he's facing away, staring off into the distance where there is nothing but black ocean.

"Captain?" I ask, pausing at the door after Miri goes inside. "Excuse me, sir?"

He doesn't answer me. I walk to the upper deck and place my hand on his arm where it rests against the railing. He startles, turning quickly to face me, his face contorted and angry.

I squeak out a soft yelp of surprise and step back.

"Are you all right?" I ask him. We've barely interacted with the crew. They're very good at staying out of sight. I imagine this is at Vincent's request. An elitist through and through, he likely expects the crew to do their work without being seen.

The captain looks around, like he's trying to make sense of his surroundings, and I realize the look on his face isn't one of anger, but fear. His eyes are glazed over, and I worry for a moment that he's been drinking, but then he blinks and they clear.

It's more like he was sleepwalking. I can see the precise moment when he remembers himself. As if I've woken him from a nightmare.

"Quite all right, thank you. You really shouldn't be up here at night, dear. It's very dangerous in the dark."

"Of course. I'm sorry."

I leave him on the upper deck and join Miri, who is waiting for me inside.

"Everything okay?" she asks.

I want to tell her no, it isn't okay, but I don't know if anything was wrong. Captain Wilson was probably just distracted, lost in thought, and I startled him.

"It's fine," I say for lack of a better response.

Miri walks beside me down the narrow hall where our rooms are, passing her own and pausing at my door with me.

"You didn't wake the others."

"No," Miri says. "I didn't."

"Why?"

"Because I'm sorry about earlier. I think I was rude. I know I was. It's just . . . I've been running in these circles with these people for so long, sometimes I forget how terrible they are. I start to become just like them. And then someone like you comes along and it's like I wake up again and remember myself."

I lean against the doorframe, watching Miri in the half-light from my room, enshrined against the hallway's darkness.

"So, I guess it was an apology. Or maybe a thank-you. For the wake-up call. I'll try not to be so obnoxious from here on out."

"It's fine, Miri."

"Don't do that."

"Do what?" I ask.

"Pacify me. Excuse my behavior. I don't need you to protect my ego; I promise it's nice and strong and thriving."

"Okay," I say. "You were kind of a brat earlier. But I do get it. I wouldn't want to be locked into the same role forever, either."

Volatile. Occasionally violent. Uninterested in making social connections.

"Thank you," Miri says. "I love it when people call me a brat to my face."

"This isn't the first time?" I ask.

"I've got an older sister, you know. And she can be downright mean when she's in a mood."

From what I'd observed on the trip so far, Effie Knight was always in a mood.

It's as though Miri can read the thought on my face, because she laughs aloud and does that thing again where she claps her own hand over her mouth. Once again, I cannot stand how cute it is. But I think she would loathe me if I even implied it. She just said in the kitchen that she hates that she's perceived that way. So I don't tell her, even though I can't stop thinking it.

"Just say you'll be honest with me, okay?"

"Fine, yes. I will be honest."

"Swear it," she demands, like a petulant child.

"Cross my heart," I say, actually drawing an X with my fingers over my chest for good measure. It has the desired effect of making Miri laugh again.

"Effie and I did that as little girls. Wasn't there a rhyme to go with it?"

"I think so. *Cross my heart, hope to die.*"

"*Stick a needle in my eye,*" she finishes. "How dramatic. But thank you for your promise. I simply abhor liars."

"Oh, you *abhor* them, do you? Did you climb out of a Jane Austen novel?"

"Hush, you," Miri says, poking at my ribs.

"*Hush up, you brash American,*" I mock her in a terrible English accent. "You know, you don't have to go out of your way to sound pretentious, Miri. You're a famous actress, for god's sake."

I expect Miri to laugh again, but her face falls at my words.

"You're right. That did sound pretentious," she says. "Thank you for saying that."

"Wait, Miri, I didn't mean—"

"No, I'm serious, Liv. I've been protected from things my whole life. First by my parents, and Effie, then my agent, and my manager. They all act like they need white gloves when they're near me. Like I'm a delicate thing to be handled. It's infuriating. I just want the truth. I can handle it."

The truth is that I have brought chaos with me like it's been my shadow my entire life. I never make the right choices. I never make the right friends. I'm a foster runaway and I stole my sister's identity just to get this far.

Of course, I can't tell Miri Knight any of that. I can't take back the lies I told to get here.

"Thank you, by the way, for waking me up," I tell her instead. "That was everything I needed tonight. To feel like maybe I'm supposed to be here."

"You're supposed to be here, Liv. I think we'll need you to keep us all in line. I'll see you tomorrow."

I watch her walk down the hall to her own room, her bare legs glowing orange in the running lights along the floor.

She gives me a wave before she disappears through her door.

I leave the light on and crawl back into my bed, pulling the blanket tight and over my head, but it doesn't work anymore. I'm no longer a child hiding from the dark. Now I'm hiding from all the little hurts that have ever happened to me, and all the harm I did in return. I'm hiding from secrets and lies.

Most nights I can make my mind go blank, like a chalkboard that's been wiped down with a wet washcloth, so you can't even see the ghosts of words left on it anymore. But tonight, I feel the marks of my past across my body, from the scar at my hairline to those on my arms, and way down deep to the ones I've locked away inside of me.

Despite Vincent's promises, the humpback whales on that first night are the only ones we see. When he complains about this after dinner, Miri shoots me a conspiring look and touches her fingertip to her lips discreetly.

Rosa has cleared the coffee table and chairs out of the living area and is using the space to teach Paris how to dance.

"I know how to dance," Paris complains when Rosa turns on the salsa music and pulls her from her cozy place on the couch with Celia.

"Not like this, you don't. My *abuela* taught me this when I was a girl. She said if you aren't feeling the music down in your soul, you aren't really dancing. None of those memorized routines you do onstage. Like *this*." Rosa laughs and pulls Paris toward her, putting her hands on her hips to forcefully move them the right way.

Paris turns as Rosa pushes, and they trip over each other's feet, landing in a twisted mess of limbs on the floor. Rosa is laughing so hard she can't breathe.

Vincent turns in his chair to watch Rosa and Paris. His gaze lingers, a sharp, bright glint in his eyes beneath the glaze of alcohol. He's been drinking his whiskey tonight instead of champagne, and he's so drunk he sways in his chair, unable to stay upright. Rosa's sweater slipped down over her shoulder, exposing the top half of her bra and her arm. She's unaware, still laughing with Paris as they climb back to their feet to try again.

Effie stands suddenly, her body blocking Vincent's view, and she reaches for the open bottle of wine on the table.

"Let's go enjoy the rest of this under the stars," Effie says, extending her other hand in invitation to Vincent.

He ignores her offer, brushes her hand away. He shifts in his seat and then suddenly looks up from the girls, cocking his head to one side.

"Do you hear that?" he asks, his focus entirely shifted. "What is that?"

"Hear what?" Effie asks.

"Rosa!" Vincent snaps his fingers to get her attention. When she doesn't hear him over the loud music, he whistles a high, sharp note. "Turn down the music!"

Rosa lifts her phone and pauses the music. The silence is abrupt.

"That!" Vincent says triumphantly, turning back to the rest of us for confirmation. "What the hell is that?"

We all wait in the quiet, listening for whatever he hears.

There is nothing.

"Vincent," Miri says. "We don't hear it. What does it sound like?"

"I'm not sure." He stands unsteadily and staggers to the bottom of the stairs, tilting his head again to listen. "Now it's gone."

"It was probably the wind," Effie says. "It's really picked up out there."

"It wasn't the wind!" Vincent shouts. "Dammit, Ef, for once you could just listen to me."

Effie is still holding the bottle of wine, though now it's swinging loosely at her side, forgotten. When she steps toward Vincent, Miri's hand shoots out and curls around her wrist gently. "Stay with us tonight," Miri says. The look in her eyes is earnest, pleading.

Every night, Effie goes off with Vincent.

The rest of us pretend not to notice.

"Stop it, Miri," Effie says, shaking her hand off and following Vincent. They climb the stairs to the deck.

"What the hell was that about?" Celia asks from the sofa. She's got a book propped open in front of her. Celia does a better job than the rest of us at making Vincent feel unwelcome, and he has hardly said anything to her on board. Whatever charms he may have seem to be wasted on her, and she makes sure he knows it.

I've been trying to emulate that.

"It's the bloody wind!" Miri says. "What the hell else would it be? He's just drunk and an asshole. He needed to make the night all about him."

"Damn, Mir, tell us how you really feel," Celia says.

"How I really feel," Miri says, her voice low and thick from drinking. "How I feel is that it would be lovely if that strong wind out there simply swept that terrible man into the sea."

"You don't mean that, Miri," Paris says.

"I do. I mean every word. Good riddance, Mr. Bellegarde, we'll take the *Bianca* from here."

"I know he's a tosser, but you don't want him dead," Celia says.

"He's no better than a dog with two dicks, chasing down any girl he can corrupt into being with him," Miri says, slurring some of her words. She's had a lot of wine tonight, and it's showing in her candor.

I take Miri's glass and finish her wine in one gulp. She gives me an Oscar-worthy side-eye at the move but says nothing.

"I'm bored," Paris says. "Let's do something different tonight."

"Like what?" Miri asks.

"I agree," Rosa says from the floor. She's lying on her back with her hair in messy braids. "The water is too rough tonight to drink a lot. We'll be sick."

The wind really has picked up outside. I can hear the

howls, strange and mournful on the open water. I'm already feeling sick from the added jostling of the waves and pitching of the floor beneath me. The water was calmer closer to shore, and I wish we'd make our way back there now.

My one sip of Miri's wine turns sour inside of me.

"I think I'm going to bed," I say. But Miri's hand grabs ahold of my arm. Even through my long sleeves I can feel the heat of her touch. Her eyes are bright with anger when she looks at me, and I get a glimpse of just how much she detests Vincent.

In a moment, the look is gone, replaced by warmth.

"Stay, Liv. You're always disappearing at night. It's such a bore," Miri says. I open my mouth to refuse, but Miri purses her lips in a slight pout. "Please."

Just one look and she has me. From the smile starting to tug at the corner of her lips, she knows it.

"Great!" Miri pulls me along with her to the living area, hopping over Rosa on the way. "Now, what's the plan?"

The last couple of nights I'd been excusing myself just after dinner. In all my plotting and scheming to get this chance, I'd never stopped to consider how little I would have in common with the people working on a film. I never anticipated the yacht, or all this time spent in close quarters with them. I'd never considered that anyone would bother to read my application or my writing. I was supposed to be Everly, not Violet.

So I had been hiding, and Miri finally called me out on it.

"We could run lines," suggests Paris.

Miri spins on her chair, her anger forgotten, and claps her hands together. "Yes! Paris. That's perfect."

"Of course it is," Celia says, throwing her head back into the couch with an exaggerated groan.

"What is it?" I feel I've missed some inside joke.

Celia climbs off the couch, tossing her throw blanket and book to the side. "Miri has never once, in her whole life, missed a chance to perform. Trust me, I've been around for it since nursery school, when she stole the spotlight as the Star over Bethlehem in the Christmas pageant."

"The *Star*?" I laugh.

"I had a song," Miri says. "It was my first time onstage. It felt like coming home."

"Ever humble, our dear Miri," Paris says, locking her arms around Miri in a tight squeeze. "But we still love her."

Thunder rolls outside, a slow growl that builds in momentum until it's right over us. When I rise from my seat at the table to go to the living room, the floor pitches beneath me, sending me to my knees and skinning them raw on the carpet.

I grit my teeth against the stinging pain.

I look around the room. The coffee table tipped over, missing Rosa's face by mere centimeters. Paris and Celia are on the sofa, gripping each other tight.

Miri's landed on her ass.

"I think it's safe to say we've hit a storm," Miri says, climbing back to her feet.

"Is it dangerous?" I ask. I've never even been in a paddle-boat before, let alone a yacht on the open sea.

"Not at all," she says, waving a hand to dismiss the idea. Then she smiles. "What do you know about *The Tempest*, Liv?" Miri asks me.

"Not very much, honestly. Only from what we read in lit class."

"You've never seen it performed onstage? What is the American education system coming to . . . Shakespeare's work isn't meant to be *read*; it is meant to be *watched*."

"Oh god, here we go," Rosa says. "Before this voyage is over, she'll have performed the entire thing for you, Liv. She's such a Shakespeare snob."

"If having a sound appreciation for theater makes me a snob . . ." Miri pauses and laughs. She covers her mouth and her cheeks flush pink. Rosa is right, she is being a snob, and I promised to tell her when she did that. I open my mouth to do just that when Miri speaks first.

"Okay, I've just actually heard what I said, and I'll admit to sounding a teeny bit full of myself." Miri pinches her fingers together to show us just how minuscule her conceit is. "But that doesn't mean I'm wrong!"

"Do you want me to get my script, Mir? It's down the hall," Rosa offers, doing a stretch as she rises from the floor to join us on the sofa.

"Thanks, but I'm good. I've been off-book for two weeks," Miri says.

Miri can't see it, but Rosa rolls her eyes at her as she walks toward us to curl up on the end of the couch.

"What part is she doing?" I whisper to Paris, but she only shushes me. Miri is already starting.

"If by your art, my dearest father, you have
Put the wild waters in this roar, allay them.
The sky, it seems, would pour down stinking pitch,
But that the sea, mounting to the welkin's cheek,
Dashes the fire out."

I won't admit it, but Miri was right about watching the work performed instead of reading it. Miri gives the words a kind of gravity they'd never have on paper alone. From Miri's lips, in its purest form, it is poetry.

"Oh, I have suffered
With those that I saw suffer! A brave vessel,
Who had no doubt some noble creature in her,
Dashed all to pieces. Oh, the cry did knock
Against my very heart! Poor souls, they perished."

When she's done, we sit in silence for a moment, sort of digesting it. I'm embarrassed to notice that I've got tears welling in my eyes, and I quickly blink them away. That's the second time one of Miri Knight's performances has made me cry. Miri is watching me too closely for her to have missed it. Her eyes are fixed only on me, even as the others cheer her performance.

There is something about the way Miri is looking at me that makes me feel like I've got to pull the blanket in tighter around my shoulders. It makes me want to pull it over my head, because Miri sees me. I think maybe she sees right through me. Like somehow she knows all my secrets.

I open my mouth to tell her how good she was when a scream wrenches through the ship from above.

"Effie!" Miri takes off running for the stairs. The rest of us are right behind her, slipping on our own socks on the slick stairs as we dash up them onto the pitching deck.

It's raining sheets of water, the downpour distorting everything.

Effie and Vincent stand at the stern of the ship. Effie is soaking wet and pale, gesturing wildly at Vincent.

"What happened?" Miri shouts over the terrible noise of the storm breaking over us.

"He jumped!" Effie says, choking on a sob. "Captain Wilson jumped off the ship!"

I feel a weight like a stone drop into my stomach. I run to the railing of the stern and look over, but there is nothing. Nothing but violent black waves crashing against the sides of the ship.

The door to the cockpit swings open, and the chief officer, Jacob, emerges, his body no more than a blur as he dashes through the rain toward us. He leans over the edge right next to me, and this close I can see the anguish on his face.

It's his father. Captain Wilson is his father. I forgot that they're related.

"What the hell was he thinking?" Jacob shouts.

"I don't know," Vincent answers. "He watched the storm rolling in. He muttered some nonsense about how beautiful it was, and then he jumped!"

"There!" Jacob shouts. "There he is."

He's right. The captain is struggling in the waves. Jacob throws a life buoy over, but Wilson sinks back into the waves before it reaches him.

"Dammit," Jacob says.

Before anyone can stop him, he climbs over the back railing and dives into the sea.

"Don't!" I scream, too late.

Jacob surfaces once and begins to swim for the last place we saw Wilson. It's obvious that he is a strong swimmer. The waves must be brutal, but he overcomes them at first, heading straight for the place he last saw his father in the waves.

But he isn't strong enough.

No one could be. Not in this. We are all screaming for him to turn back. To grab the life buoy that is now several yards behind him. He crests the next wave, and then, just like his father, he's gone.

Vincent runs to the cockpit, and I can hear him shouting on the radio. After a few minutes, Effie joins him inside, pulling the door shut behind her.

The rest of us stand in the freezing rain, staring at the place where the men vanished into the waves. My hands are clinging too tight to the railing, and they've lost all the blood in them. I shake them to get it back and feel pins and needles creep into my palms and fingertips. Miri is beside me. She pulls one of my hands into hers without a word.

There is rain pouring down her face, but there are tears too.

I don't know how I can tell the difference, but I can.

When we realize they aren't coming back, we return to the living quarters below. Ms. Simmons is there waiting with hot tea for everyone. She slips around the room, quietly pressing warm mugs into our frozen hands. She brings tissues around for the tears.

An hour later, Effie joins us. She's drenched, shivering, but pushes Miri away when she brings a blanket to her.

"We didn't say anything before," Effie says. "There was no point, not until it was fixed."

"Effie?" Paris asks, stepping closer, pressing her own tea into Effie's hands, and then bringing it to Effie's mouth so she'll take a sip.

Effie drinks, then clears her throat and looks up at the rest of us. "Earlier tonight we lost all communications. Wilson couldn't receive any messages, nor could he send any out. There are backup systems for situations like this, redundancies, beacons for emergencies. None of them were working."

"But they're working now, right, Effie?" Miri asks.

"No," Effie says. "They're not."

The lights flicker around us, flashing once. Then again. And then they go off.

We've lost power.

"Liv."

It doesn't feel like morning when I open my eyes to darkness.

We've slept in the living room together, piled on top of each other on the sofa. Anything to not feel alone as the storm raged. None of us could sleep, until Effie opened a bottle of wine, passing it around so we could take turns drinking.

It wasn't until we finished a second bottle that we finally drifted off, too drunk and sad—too tired of being scared—to stay awake any longer.

"*Liv,* wake up. Something's wrong."

My stomach churns from all the wine, and I know I'm going to be sick. But it isn't just my stomach rolling, it's the entire ship. The storm has grown worse in the hours we slept.

I wake fully and sit up. I can barely make out Paris in the darkness—her pink hair has the slightest glimmer. I reach for a phone, not mine, but it doesn't matter. It's past six in the morning and unnaturally dark outside the windows of the ship. I check for service, just in case, but there's nothing. We haven't had service on our phones since the second day at sea.

"Hurry," Paris says, pulling on my arm until I stand with her.

We'd only had two or three precious hours of sleep. I'm confident I'm still drunk.

I start to follow Paris toward the stairs when suddenly the floor falls away beneath me, and for a moment I'm floating. The ship lands hard when it comes down from the wave, and I slam into the ground. My shoulder strikes the edge of the mirrored coffee table with a sharp crack.

I hope it was the table breaking and not my bone.

Blood flows freely down my arm, warm and wet. It hurts like hell, but I can't tell how serious it is through the haze of alcohol. I swear I'll never drink again.

The nausea wins the next round, and I throw up across the plush white carpet.

I wipe my mouth on the blanket abandoned on the floor nearby, the only thing within reach, and try to cover up the vomit with it.

"Forget it, Liv. It doesn't matter. We need you out here."

I spot my sweatshirt under the galley table and tug it on, wincing as I lift my injured arm to get it through the sleeve. I press my other hand hard against the cut, trying as best I can to slow the bleeding. Then I stumble after Paris, bracing myself against the walls on either side of the steps, pushing myself up every time there is a lull in the thrashing of our ship.

The scene I emerge to is one from mythology. The ocean is vicious around us, black and churning and desperate. Like it's thirsty for us. I imagine how it will feel to sink down into its darkness, closing in around me, pressure building until I break and suck in salt water instead of air.

I'm soaked through instantly by freezing rain and the waves lapping up over the sides of the yacht. Paris has my hand, and she's pulling me onward, up to the deck with the cockpit. In a flash of lightning, I can see silhouettes inside, all huddled together.

But I'm disoriented by the pitching of the ship, the lingering alcohol, the white-hot pain in my shoulder. Each step takes a lifetime and a herculean effort, even with Paris helping me.

The sky and the sea compete in their violence, tossing the ship like a toy in a bath. No more than a plaything meant to be destroyed.

We finally make it to the upper deck, where the other girls have crowded into the enclosed cockpit, Vincent scrambling with the radio, clutching the handset so tight his knuckles are white. Effie is kneeling on the ground, plugging wires into ports. Vincent turns a dial frantically, his shouting barely audible over the chaos of the storm.

"MAYDAY! MAYDAY!"

But when he releases the button, there's only silence. Not even static or the crackle of radio coming through. Communications are still down. The power is still gone.

We aren't going to make it.

I reach for the life jackets that line the walls, handing them off as fast as I can to the others. We are frantic, trying to figure out the straps and buckles in the dark. There are extra vests still left on the wall, meant for Captain Wilson and his son and Ms. Simmons, who never emerged from the living quarters.

The boat crests another huge wave, and there's a brilliant flash of lightning, blinding white, but for a moment, I see something rising from the ocean, its shape imprinted on my vision when the light fades.

"Look, there's land!" I yell. My words are swallowed by the wind. I wave wildly at the darkness, and Miri looks where I'm pointing, but the island is gone in the dark. Another wave rolls beneath us, and the ship crashes downward. We fall into each other like pawns on a chessboard at the mercy of some invisible, vengeful hand.

"Help," Miri gasps when I am pressed up against her. She gestures to her back, where her hair has caught on something. I try to pull her loose, but it's knotted so tight it's futile. I can't get it free without tearing her hair out of her head.

I search for something sharp.

Vincent's keys dangle from his belt loop, and I reach for them. I don't bother to unhook them, I just pull, tearing the belt loop of his pants. I slip the key into her hair and tug hard.

It gives way. Though I leave a sizable bit of her hair stuck there, she is free. When she falls against me, I can feel how fast she's breathing. She's panicking. Hyperventilating.

My hand finds her chest, and our eyes meet. I place my other hand on my own chest and show her the steady rise and fall. Slowly, slowly. *Breathe.*

Miri calms her breathing, and we have to work to pull ourselves back to standing, fighting the chaotic rocking beneath us. We grip anything we can reach on the wall for balance. I wonder if this is why Wilson jumped. Maybe he knew it was coming. Maybe he knew it was hopeless.

Vincent is still screaming into the radio, but I have no idea if anything is getting through.

I look out into the storm, and I see something in the water. It is moving fast and heading our way. This wave is unlike the others. It is massive, like a wall of water.

A rogue wave.

I'd seen one before, though it was smaller than this. We were on the beach with Rachel, during our last spring break. The surf had been rough all day, and we were standing back from the shore when one wave came in faster and stronger than all the rest. It swept up against the rocks, knocking people off their feet, pulling them back toward the ocean with its force. It was fast and massive and seemed to come from nowhere. Just like this one now.

There is barely time to react. I pull Miri back down so we are crouching beneath the navigation board. Before I can even call a warning to the others, the wave hits.

The ship rolls. Once. Twice.

We hit something massive and unmovable. Rock jutting out from the ocean, and I remember the island, and something like hope blooms within me in the moment before the glass windows explode. Bodies crash onto us and the cockpit floods with water.

A resounding *crack* comes from deep within the belly of the ship. Vincent's coveted yacht starts to break in half around us.

All I know in the darkness is a hand in mine, belonging, impossibly, to a girl I'd once watched from afar, and now would die with. We are lost, pummeled by water on every side, and I don't know which way it is to the surface, and which way to a certain death by drowning. Then Miri's hand is torn from my grasp, and there is only darkness.

Just after six in the morning, on its third day at sea, Vincent Bellegarde's luxury yacht wrecks somewhere off the coast of Alaska, in the freezing waters of the northern Pacific Ocean, and with no means of communication.

The *Bianca* goes under with eight souls still on board.

I'm vomiting before I'm even fully awake.

My throat and nose burn from the caustic mix of salt water and wine. I need to roll over. My face is pressed into sand and water laps at my face, washing away my sickness but also trying earnestly to drown me.

The ache is everywhere. Every muscle in my shoulders and thighs and even my wrists protest the movement as I twist my hands to dig into the sand and silt beneath me. It is a wrenching, pained movement that flips my body over, and I cough violently as I suck in air. I close my eyes against the sky's brightness.

The next wave crashes over me whole, drenching me, and I'm spitting out more salt water even as I try to move backward, farther onto the shore. *There was an island.*

I open my eyes and find dark pine trees all around, crowding my vision in a world turned upside down. Trees above and a patch of overcast sky below. The roaring ocean is all around and somehow inside of me, too, crashing and pulling me back under again.

I remember a scratchy pillowcase pressed tight against my face to suffocate me. I remember the way running out of oxygen feels like a dark cloud rolling in, ready to steal away your consciousness forever. I'm afraid that if I close my eyes again, I'll pass out. I'll drown right here in the shallows.

I dig my elbows into the earth and use them to shift up and away from the waves. I'm not sure how long it takes me to move a few yards, just beyond the reach of the water, but I know that every inch is hard-fought, a battle I didn't know I had in me for how exhausted I am.

The urge to survive comes from somewhere deep within as I claw my way out of death's tightening grip once more.

Finally, I no longer feel water at my feet, and I collapse back onto pebbles and sand.

When I wake again, the light is blinding. The storm has passed, and I blink against the brightness of the sun directly overhead. It's around midday, but I don't know which day. I can't tell how much time has passed. All I know is that I've never been so thirsty in my life. My throat is raw, my lips cracked, my tongue so dry inside my mouth that it feels like a foreign object.

Sitting up doesn't feel like an option, so I start smaller. I wiggle my toes. Or at least I think I do. I try to lift my head to check, but my neck is too stiff and hurts with the effort. For a while I lie there, gathering my strength—or perhaps just the sheer willpower—to try to move again.

I notice a tickling sensation on my hand, and turn toward it. This movement is easier. I can swivel my head to the side and look at my right arm, outstretched across the silty beach.

A large blue crab perches in the sand.

I watch as one pincer reaches out to my fingertip. My skin is macerated, wet and soggy, across the soft pads of my fingers. The crab grips the edge of the softened skin and pulls, tearing a piece loose and drawing it to its mouth.

It is eating me.

That's when I notice more of that same tickling sensation. On my left shoulder, and the bottoms of my feet. At my knee, where the denim is torn open. When I look to my other side, I find more crabs perched all around me, consuming me.

When I throw up this time, I begin to choke, still lying flat on my back, and it takes everything I've got to roll back over again so I don't asphyxiate.

The crabs scatter at the movement—I hear the rhythmic staccato of dozens of legs striking against rock as they scuttle back to their tide pools and the safety of the water. I pull my arms in first, hiding my vulnerable fingers, and then slowly draw my knees beneath me, too.

I need to move. I need water. There is a pain throbbing

behind and above my right eye. Steady as a heartbeat, thudding away inside my skull so hard I shut that eye against it. I don't think I hit my head when we wrecked, though I can't be sure. The headache could just be from dehydration.

Slowly, I rise to my feet.

My shoulder is throbbing with pain, too. I reach my arm across my body to the blood-soaked part of my sweatshirt. It has dried, stuck to the cut.

I pull the sweatshirt down from my neck, stretching the material to its limit to get a closer look at the injury. The fabric pulls at my skin, and I grit my teeth as it starts to give way, bleeding again, though not as bad as before.

The gash is deep across my upper arm. There is a bit of white bone visible, and when I try to move it, I see my own muscle ripple inside the wound. I hold my breath against the pain and look away. If there was anything left inside of me, I'd be getting sick again, but there's nothing at all.

Dry heaving hurts even worse.

It's a rough injury, but not a fatal one. It isn't even bleeding much, just cracked wide open, exposed and awful to look at. So I don't look at it.

Move, Liv.

My legs surprise me by obeying the command, and I start to stumble down the beach. The remnants of the *Bianca* are visible in the waves, just barely. Part of it is smashed against the rocky coast of the island. The rest must be underwater.

"Hello!" I call out, but the sound is hoarse and hollow. No one would hear it over the roar of the ocean on the shore.

A few minutes later, I spy a flash of color in the monotonous sand. A vibrant violet among all the gray and brown.

Rosalind.

In my hurry, I trip, falling to my knees and catching myself, sending a wave of pain up through my injured shoulder. But I look up to see a wave crashing over Rosa, and I climb to my feet, ignoring how much it hurts.

When I reach Rosa, I have to fight to get her hair off of her face. Her lips are a brilliant shade of blue. She is leaning against one of the large outcroppings of rock making up the shoreline, not submerged, but drenched. I press my ear against her chest, reaching for her wrist at the same time.

Thump . . . thump. A pulse. It is weak, and it is slow. But it's there. Rosa is breathing.

"Rosa!" I try to wake her. "Rosalind!"

I hook my good arm around her chest and pull her away from the water. She's so cold, I can't believe she's alive.

My sweatshirt is mostly dry, and I peel it off my body, a painstakingly slow process as I navigate my hurt shoulder. I yank the fabric over Rosa's head and down her torso. I don't bother to get her hands through the sleeves—I tuck them against her chest for added warmth and tie the sleeves around her tight. I make sure she is propped up safely against a boulder away from the water. Rosa's condition is more dire than mine. We need help, soon, or she'll die.

I set off down the beach.

My legs are shaking so badly I have to stop frequently and lean against the branches of the massive pine trees lining the shoreline.

But my efforts are rewarded when I see someone far ahead.

"Hey!" I shout and wave. "Hey!"

The person standing on the beach starts to run toward me, her red hair loose and wild in the breeze.

"Liv," Effie says when she gets close. "Thank god you're all right."

My arms are folded across my chest, and my teeth are chattering.

"Rosa is back there," I manage. "She's not awake. Freezing cold. Must have been in the water a long time."

"The others are this way," Effie says, and slips her arm into mine, pulling me along the beach. "I'll get you to them and then we'll go back for Rosa."

"Who is . . . there?" I ask. The word *alive* was right there, perched on the tip of my tongue, but I couldn't say it. Speaking the word *alive* out loud felt like beckoning the word *dead,* and I wasn't ready for that yet.

"Paris, Celia, and Vincent."

That means Miri is missing. Or not missing, if they already found her body. The thought fills me with panic, and I try to focus on my body and its movements, its more subtle aches as well as the tight, insistent pain in my shoulder. I try to count the breaths filling my lungs. But I can't block out her voice, stuck in my head from last night, repeating like a skipping record. *Dashed all to pieces. Poor souls, they perished,* Miri had said. Her voice had been sure and steady, speaking the words into existence like an enchantress.

I'm grateful for Effie's support as we walk the shore, though it's only a few minutes before I see the others. They are huddled up, flanks close, like a pile of nesting birds.

"Liv!" Celia rises to her feet when we get close and throws her arms around me. I'm surprised by the affection for only a second, and then I wrap my arms around her, too.

"I'm so glad you're okay," Celia says. "Well, not okay. I know it's not okay."

"I know what you mean," I tell her.

Paris gets up from the sand and puts her hand on my arm. I twist my wrist ever so slightly, even though my scars are the least important thing right now. They're always at the forefront of my brain, waiting for someone to ask the questions I dread.

"We're missing Rosa and Miri," Paris says.

"Not Rosa," Effie says. "I need help getting her. Liv said she's unconscious up the beach."

"What about the other crew member? The chef?" I ask. The woman had been handing us mugs of hot tea just a few hours ago. She wasn't on deck when the ship split. She was probably in her room. Maybe she found a life jacket in time.

"There's been no sign of her, either," Effie says.

"Liv, stay here and rest," Celia says. "And keep an eye on Vincent."

"Why?" I ask, my eyes finally finding the only real adult among us. He is sitting on the sand, eyes vacant and staring at the ocean.

"He's not doing so great," Effie says.

"Is he hurt?" I ask.

"We don't think so. Just in shock, I guess. He hasn't said a word."

The others head back the way we came to get Rosalind. A few minutes later, Vincent stands slowly and walks closer to the water. He reaches into his deep pockets and pulls out a soggy cigar, placing it between his lips.

From his other pocket he pulls a lighter.

He holds it up, flicks it once, twice. The little flame lights, and he holds it uselessly against the wet cigar.

I step forward and pluck the lighter from his hands.

"We can *use* this. To build a fire." He doesn't protest, doesn't acknowledge me, so I leave him at the water's edge and head for the tree line. I gather small dead twigs and bits of dried leaves. It's summer, though, and almost everything is wet and lush. It is hard to find things to burn.

I try to break off some of the lower branches from a pine tree, but every muscle in my body aches, and my shoulder is throbbing. I give up after the second one snaps off, sending white-hot pain ricocheting up my arm like a bullet.

Back on the beach I gather what I managed to find into a little pile and hold the lighter against the edges. *Please, please work.* A flicker. A leaf catches and immediately sizzles and goes out. Dammit. Too wet. And my clothes are still damp with ocean water. Everly used to talk about this, about how vital knowing how to start a fire was, and I always ignored her. If she were here now, she'd know exactly what to do.

I'm too tired to laugh at the irony.

But then I remember something from one of the documentaries she was always watching. In a pinch, with no dry tinder, human hair can be used. It's highly combustible.

I reach for my own hair, hanging in snarls around my shoulders. I pull strands out a few at a time, ignoring each pinch against my scalp. When I have a small pile of hair, I roll it until it tangles even more, into a little mouse nest of a ball. It's disgusting, and perfect.

I set it on top of my pile of leaves and twigs and try the lighter again, hovering over the mess I've made to shield it from the breeze.

The hair catches fire, and it burns hot and fast. I manage to move some of the leaves to the top of it, and they start to burn, too. I blow on it gently until a thin trail of smoke rises from the scraps, followed by a bright orange tendril of flame.

It's the most beautiful thing I've ever seen.

I hurry to feed more leaves and brush to the pile, building the kindling, feeding the fire carefully. I hold my hands up to the promise of warmth and wait for feeling to creep back into my fingertips, still bloody and raw from the cut and the water and the crabs.

"Impressive," says a voice above me, and I find a pale face half hidden behind a ripple of matted blond hair. Miri.

"You're alive," I whisper, rising to my feet. She doesn't look injured, just exhausted, and like the rest of us, a near miss from hypothermia's clutches.

"Considering the circumstances, maybe we should go with 'You're not dead yet,'" Miri says, reaching out. She takes my hand in hers and smiles, but it's nothing like before. Before, her smile seemed genuine. Like she was lit from within.

This smile is mournful, and with her last words echoing in my mind, I know why. *Living* can be a burden. I know that better than most.

Instead of drowning, we are here, and we are all very much alive. Now we make the decision to try to survive for however long it takes for us to get off of this island.

Unfortunately, our collective skills for living in the wilderness likely hover just above the threshold of *nothing.* Not a quick death at sea, but a slow one, here.

Not dead yet.

Miri and I stand there facing each other, our fingertips

barely hooked together between us. I'm certain we share the same look reflected in our eyes, one of fear. One of bereavement. But we aren't mourning what's already been lost to us.

We are grieving what comes next.

Rosa is still unconscious when the sun begins to set. We've put her beside the fire, which is now blazing hot on the beach, fed by branches and more dried leaves that we scoured the beach and woods to find.

Celia helps me tear the hem off the bottom of my shirt and wrap it around the gash on my shoulder. If the grotesqueness of it bothers her, she doesn't let on. She finishes quickly, tucking the edges in tight. It isn't exactly clean, but it's better than leaving the deep wound exposed.

"Thank you," I tell her. "I couldn't even look at it again."

"It's ghastly," Celia says. "We need to watch for infection, right?"

Infection seems like a foregone conclusion given the circumstances.

Rosa had been wearing several layers of clothes when the ship capsized. Long sleeves and then a sweatshirt overtop. Jeans with flared bottoms, capable of soaking up plenty of water. It was all too heavy, too bulky. And she hadn't gotten her life jacket secured before the wreck. Rosa probably only survived because she was an athlete. She made it to shore, but only barely, and at a great cost. Her exhaustion is absolute.

I find a blanket washed up in one of the tide pools, shimmering lavender beneath the surface of the water. It's covered in a handful of hermit crabs and pink starfish, clinging to the material like ornaments. I clean it off best I can and lay it out on the rocks near the fire. Once it is dry, we pull it around Rosa's body. Then the five of us take turns holding her, providing what little body heat we can.

Eventually the drawn paleness of her face starts to warm to its normal tone, and light blooms of pink appear on her cheeks. Her lips are chapped, raw and red, but it's still so much better than the deadly blue they'd been when I first found her.

Lined up against a rock are the other items that washed ashore all afternoon from the shipwreck. Fourteen water bottles. A few cans of soda. A jagged piece of metal from the hull of the ship. And lastly, the dislocated speaker from the radio that Vincent had been yelling into uselessly when the ship went under. Its long cord is intact, but the speaker itself is smashed, with exposed, frayed wires among the bits of black plastic.

And that's it. That's all we have.

"Hey, on the bright side, if we survive this, it will be one hell of a story," Celia says from across the fire. Paris is beside her, head lolling on her shoulder where she's drifted off. As I watch, she shivers violently, and Celia's arm wraps around her, pulling her in tight, letting her head slip down to rest in Celia's lap instead.

It's nice that they have each other. That they aren't alone in this place. Though I bet either of them would wish the other was someplace safe, given the chance.

"It's already a story," I say. "Which is good. People will care, and they will look."

For all of you, I think, but don't bother to say out loud.

Our situation is dire, but it isn't hopeless. I look around the fire at the faces I've seen on film and in music videos and on the Olympic platform awaiting a gold medal. They will have people looking for them. People with money, and resources, and maybe even a governor's phone number or two.

Vincent is wandering around. His movements seem aimless—he's not collecting bits of wood for the fire or searching for pieces of the wreck. In fact, Vincent hasn't done a single useful thing all day. The only person he's spoken to is Effie, in the same hushed murmurs they'd used on the yacht, when they'd stand apart from the group.

Effie and Miri sit on the other side of the fire, facing the sea. The sun is setting, and despite everything, I have to admit that it is like nothing I've ever seen. A thousand shades of pink and orange streak across the sky. The gradient grows into deep purple clouds right above us.

When I turn back to the fire, I find Rosa's eyes are open where she's lying on her side on the mix of pebble and silt and sand that makes up the shoreline. Her brown eyes are wide, her pupils dilated in the dying light. Her cheeks hollowed out by hours of dehydration. She looks skeletal, an impression that becomes even more pronounced by the first words out of her mouth.

"Are we dead?" she asks. She doesn't move or try to sit up. She doesn't even look around to take in our surroundings before she asks the question.

"No," I tell her. "We're fine." I reach for one of the water bottles from our limited supply and pass it to Miri, who helps Rosa up so she can drink. We'll have to ration everything, but even so, it won't last long. If we don't find fresh water soon, we'll have days, not weeks. Certainly not however long it will take rescuers to find our last point of navigation and figure out we landed here.

Rosa only sips at the water. Miri wordlessly urges her to continue, but Rosa lifts her hands in protest. "Don't. I'll get sick. We shouldn't waste it on me." As she talks, her lips crack open, both top and bottom, and begin bleeding.

She licks the blood away.

I hold up the lighter that I confiscated from Vincent.

"This should last us a while if we're careful with it, but we should try to keep a signal fire burning at all times."

"What's a signal fire?" Effie is turned around now, holding her hands palms-first to the heat. The firelight shimmers across the red of her hair, turning it almost bronze in the glow. Even now, she looks like she belongs on a stage with a spotlight framing her face.

Instead, she is here. Where none of us belong.

"We want to make sure that rescuers see some sign of life on the island. Especially if they're passing by at night or overhead. We don't even know if this island is charted anywhere; it might be really small. We ought to explore it tomorrow once we've had some rest. Our priority is going to be fresh water, and then food."

For tonight, I've rationed us two water bottles, split six ways. I gave Vincent his own, in part because I'm worried he might just keel over dead from shock soon, and also because the less we have to deal with him, the better.

"How do you know all of this?" Effie leans forward. She seems to be the most put-together out here. She sips her allocated one-third of a water bottle and passes it on, eager to listen to what I have to say.

"My sister really likes hiking and camping and wilderness stuff. Last year she did this survivalist training program, and she told me about some of it."

"Well, that's helpful," Paris says. She's awake again but

hasn't moved from Celia's lap, seeming to prefer the closeness of their position. Celia strokes her hair absentmindedly.

"It would be more helpful if I'd listened to her and gone along." I shrug it off, but I'm imagining Everly now. I wonder if the news has broken. I wonder what she'll think when the news reports her name instead of mine. I wonder if it's possible that she could hate me more than she already did. "But I remember some things, at least. She talked about this stuff a lot."

"Cheers to that. It might keep us alive out here until rescue comes." Celia drinks her portion of the water slowly, closing her eyes and savoring it.

"Vincent!" Effie calls out. He is nothing but a silhouette against the last streaks of bloodred and violet sky behind him. A shadow against the growing darkness.

He turns toward us and surprises me when he jogs over. He half falls into the sand beside Effie.

"Effie, dear. My darling Ophelia. You *are* my favorite."

Effie's eyebrows lower at his words, and I realize it isn't a compliment. Paris looks away, embarrassed for her.

"My other lovers are real pieces of work, but not you, dear girl. *You* are sweet."

Something has brought out Vincent's Southern accent in full force. The trauma, I guess, or perhaps just not caring to keep up the facade of having a certain kind of background. Everyone knew that Vincent grew up on a ranch in Texas, but it was never a real focus in the tabloids. They talked about his girlfriends, his ex-wives, his children—a few of whom are probably older than Effie. They talked about his elite theater degree from Yale. It only dawns on me now that this was all by design. Not an accident, but a facet of him that was shaped by the best publicists that money could find.

"Effie, love, do you hear it now? Do you hear the angel's voice? She's calling me."

Vincent leans over, reaching for Effie's hand. She wrenches it away.

"Please don't touch me," she says. "Don't act like you care. You've done nothing to help us all day."

"Hey, Effie," I say, preparing to defend him. People react to trauma in all kinds of ways, and not all of them are particularly useful. And it sounds like Vincent is hallucinating or has a head injury if he is hearing things.

"And aren't you a useful little thing." Vincent turns to me now that I started to defend him. "And real pretty, too. Do you know that?"

"That doesn't matter," I say.

"Doesn't it?"

"Not for anything good."

"Ah, well, maybe I spoke too soon," Vincent drawls. "But you're right. It doesn't matter. Not out here. We're all going to die anyway. No one knows where we are."

"How long were communications down?" I ask. I thought

it was only a few hours at the most.

"The trouble isn't the communications, darling." Vincent's drawl is thick, this time with cruelty instead of alcohol. "No one knew about our little whale excursion."

"What?" Paris asks.

"They'll look in all the wrong places. We were so far off the course I submitted. I told Wilson I amended it, but I lied. It's hopeless, really, if we're honest about it." The words are more than a heavy blow. They're a death sentence. But Vincent delivers them slowly, with an air of casualness that makes me want to strangle him.

"Vincent, why would you do that?" Celia demands.

"I was only being a good host. It was meant to be an adventure," he drawls out.

Vincent looks around the fire at our shocked faces.

He starts to laugh. The first bark of it startles me so much I jump. He laughs hard, and it seems to go on forever. Not a practiced, polished laugh reserved for films or parties filled with producers and directors, but his real laugh. It is incessant, jarring in these circumstances, and it keeps going on and on.

"It doesn't matter, Effie, *love*. I really should be looking at this as a boon. Just me and all these beautiful girls."

"Beautiful, beautiful girls who want absolutely *nothing* to do with you, Vincent," Rosa says, her voice dripping venom from where she is still lying prone on the sand. Like a viper ready to strike at his slightest provocation.

"And *you* probably won't make it to morning," Vincent says nastily in response.

The outcry from all of us is immediate. He'd gone too far. We really don't know if Rosa will make it. But for Vincent to say it to her so callously was cruel and unnecessary.

"Up." Effie climbs to her feet, brushing dirt and sand off herself, and gestures, demanding Vincent stand, too. "Now."

"Ah, leave me alone," Vincent says, and adds insult to injury by gulping down the rest of his full water bottle.

We all stare at him, our own throats burning with thirst.

He isn't in shock.

He's just an asshole.

"Up. Now," Effie says again. I don't know what it is about her tone this time, but I'm not even surprised when Vincent obeys.

Effie stands there with her red hair flaming, looking Vincent Bellegarde square in the eyes—she's actually a little taller than him, I realize.

"Get the hell out of here, Vincent."

"What are you talking about?"

"Go. You aren't welcome here. You can figure it out for yourself. Collect your own washed-up supplies. Forage in the woods. I don't give a damn."

"And you aren't queen of this whole godforsaken place. Wherever we are." Vincent throws up his hands. "The others want me here. For protection." Vincent looks around the fire, waiting for us to protest Effie's demand.

He is met with only the crackling fire and the lapping waves.

"Just go, Vincent," Miri says. "Go sleep off . . . whatever the hell this is. Your little meltdown. Take it somewhere else."

Vincent clenches his teeth, his jaw rippling under his stubble as he scans all our faces and finds no friends among us.

"Fine. Good luck," he snaps at us. He sets off—not down the beach like I'd expected, but straight into the dark woods. I feel like I've just watched a child throw a tantrum because he couldn't play with all the toys.

Miri catches my look and smiles at me, a quick flash and it's gone again. Blink and you'd miss it. I smile back, and it feels like a secret passes between us in the moment. Our awareness of each other, our shared sense of humor—dark humor, to find it in the face of all this awfulness.

But it *is* a little funny, to be stuck here, on the verge of death, dealing with a middle-aged movie star throwing fits because no one is giving him the attention he's used to.

I laugh softly. I catch myself and feel ashamed for a second, but then Miri laughs, too, and tries to cover it. Then Effie joins us. It isn't the same as Vincent's hearty, barking, grating laugh. It isn't full of that same mockery and defeat and desperation. His laugh was scared. It was all too aware of how terrible things were.

Celia and Paris begin to laugh, too. And softly, so quiet I nearly miss it, Rosa, too. We laugh so we aren't sobbing. We laugh to remind ourselves that we are here. We are alive, for now. But *for now* is enough. We survived Vincent Bellegarde's ineptitude with the *Bianca*. We are undrowned, and together. That has to be enough, because it's really all we've got.

A deep, loud crack of a tree limb breaking comes from the woods, silencing us in one fell swoop, like a hellkite hawk taking out a nest of baby squirrels.

The quiet is absolute. There had been bugs chirping before, and small mammals scuttling through the forest floor, and the occasional screech of an owl, but I wasn't fully aware of their noises until they stopped, all at once. The forest is suddenly, deathly quiet, for a heartbeat. Two. Three.

Then the screaming begins.

At first, I think it must be a wildcat. Or a dying rabbit. Predator or prey, it is wild and inhuman. But then I recognize a word in the screams. A name, actually, again and again.

Effie.

It is Vincent, and he's calling for her, but it's wrong, all wrong. The pain in his screams is real and it is awful. Effie springs to her feet, racing into the forest.

Miri is right behind her, but Celia tackles her to the beach.

"You can't," Celia says, her voice pleading and soft and desperate in Miri's ear. "You can't go in there."

I grab fistfuls of sand, suffocating the flames on the beach as quickly as I can. So much for a signal fire. The screaming continues, but it sounds less and less like Vincent. Less like a person as words devolve into horrible sounds. Gurgling, choking sounds.

"Hurry," I whisper, and Paris helps me loop our arms around Rosa, bringing her with us. We back away from the edge of the woods, toward the water.

The others join us, with Celia supporting Miri the same way Paris and I have got Rosa. Not because she's ill, but because she might still try to go in there after Effie. We crouch in one of the shallow tide pools, laying ourselves across the rough rocks that make up the shoreline of the island, and we wait, quiet, listening.

It doesn't last much longer. I'm grateful when it stops because I think nothing could be more terrible than those screams, but I'm wrong.

The silence is worse.

A few minutes later, there is a shuffling sound at the edge of the woods, near where our campfire had been burning. I'm surprised to notice that I'm actually trembling with fear. I always thought that was just something people said to be dramatic, but it's true. I can't keep still.

A figure emerges from the darkest part of the forest.

It's Effie.

I leave the others and rush forward. Her pajamas are dark,

the light blue covered in a large wet spot. When I reach her, I press my hand against it and pull away.

It's blood. Effie is soaked with it.

"It's not mine," she says, and collapses.

I've never been more grateful for morning.

We rest in shifts, with two of us awake at all times.

I thought it would be hard to stay up when I was so deeply exhausted, but whenever I got tired, I only had to remember the keening pitch of Vincent's final screams, and I would be alert once again, my eyes trained on the line where the beach ended and the dark of the woods began.

I have the last shift of the night, and when the sky begins to brighten, I know we've survived our first night here. The sun rises on the far side of the island, and the light comes slowly, creeping steadily over the treetops. I have no idea if we are safer in the daylight from whatever it was that we heard last night, but it feels better to leave behind that uncanny fear of the dark that I never fully outgrew. Afraid of things that move in the night.

Miri took the last shift with me, and when she drifted to sleep on my shoulder an hour ago, I let her. I was awake enough that I wasn't worried about needing her for accountability. And I liked it. I liked the way she shifted nearer to me in the dark and slipped one of her hands into mine, falling asleep against my arm. I liked that she felt safe enough to do that in this place.

The only problem is that I'm trapped, and I've had to pee for hours.

I try to move her slowly. We are beside a mass of sleeping girls. Celia and Paris are entwined, Rosa curled up beside them, with the blanket we found pulled across them. Effie is apart from the others, only by a few inches, but she must have been cold all night.

Only Rosa and I had been wearing jeans when we shipwrecked. Everyone else was wearing thin pajama bottoms and tank tops.

The blood has dried on Effie's shirt, so dark it looks black in the gray early-morning light. As I'm watching, Effie shivers, almost violently, and I lean forward, pressing my hand to her cheek. I shift the blanket, stretching the material over her shoulders and tucking it in around her.

I try to gently lean Miri toward Effie, but she startles awake, wide-eyed and scared.

"It's okay," I say, wrapping my hand around hers. "I'm here. You're okay."

There is this moment of clouded confusion, and then I see it all come back to her. The wreck. Vincent. The incident that led to us crouching in between rocks all night in soggy, sinking sands, with no protection from the wind.

The fact that it is summer, and the temperatures are mild, is the only reason we survived the night. We didn't stand a chance of finding shelter.

"Thought maybe it was all a nightmare for a second," Miri says. She notices her hand in mine, and I wait for her to pull away.

She does, but she squeezes it first. Twice.

"Thank you for letting me sleep. You didn't have to."

"I wanted to."

Miri has spots of pink in her cheeks from the wind. It gives the impression of a fever, and I move without thinking, pressing my palm to her forehead.

"Sorry," I say, pulling back like I've touched fire, and not the smooth coolness of her skin. "Thought you looked feverish."

"Just chapped cheeks, I bet. I always got them in winter as a kid. Now they don't let me stay out in the cold long enough for them."

"You don't seem the type to listen to rules," I say.

"You'd be surprised, then. The trouble is remembering them all," she says.

I do this strange thing almost every time I look at her, where I try to put together two versions of her: the perfect vision of Miri Knight I knew from watching her in movies and awards shows, and then the very normal girl sitting beside me right now.

She's just as vulnerable as I am out here. She's just as human.

I leave Miri on watch so I can sneak down the beach to pee. I keep the woods on my right as far away as possible. There is noise within—birds waking and singing. A rabbit crouched underneath some ferns. They wouldn't do that if there was a predator nearby. Even so, I hurry back to the group as fast as I can.

The others are awake when I return. Rosa looks much better today. That horrible paleness is gone from the day before, and she's drinking water.

"We should probably make a plan for the day," I say. I can't bring myself to sit on the rocks again—one night on them was enough. My muscles protest every movement today. "Try to make some kind of shelter. Find fresh water."

"In the woods?" Effie asks. The circles under her eyes look like bruises.

"Yes." We don't have a choice. We'll be out of water by tomorrow.

"I'm going with you," she says.

It isn't until she says it that I realize I'd already planned for it to be me going into the woods. But Effie definitely shouldn't go, and I hope she doesn't make me say why.

"Effie—" Miri begins, but Effie is already up, rubbing her

hands over her bare arms to warm them.

"Not arguing it, Miri. I'm going."

"All right," I say, stepping forward. "Then let's go. We need water, desperately."

I gather the empty water bottles so we have something to fill if—when—when we find water.

"Can you walk the shore while we're gone and see if anything else washed up?" I ask the others. "At some point we need to swim out to the wreck and see if there's anything salvageable."

"Yeah, we'll look," Celia says, helping Rosa to her feet.

You probably won't make it to morning.

Vincent's words are still there, hovering around us like a misread premonition.

"Be careful," Miri says behind me. I turn around, expecting her to be talking to her sister, but Miri is looking right at me.

"Oh," I say, surprised. "I will. We'll be fine."

"Swear it," Miri says, her voice just as demanding as it was on the ship, even though now it is hoarse, cracking from her thirst.

"Cross my heart," I tell her, and she smiles. I wish she'd stop asking me to make promises I'm not sure I can keep.

When Effie and I first step beneath the shadowed canopy of the forest, we pause. We both know what we're waiting for. We don't have to say it out loud.

These aren't like the woods of Southern California.

Everything here is dark and wet, shades of green so vibrant they're nearly teal in the morning glow. There isn't any direct sunlight breaking through the thick evergreen trees—trees that are mammoth compared to the ones at home—but as the sun rises, the viridian glow of the forest brightens.

When nothing awful immediately happens to us, we begin to walk.

I watch for signs of life, hoping it will tell me where we are. We are far enough north that the climate is temperate, not tropical. The trees are massive pines, not swaying palms. The coast is black silted sand and rocks, not white crystalline beaches. We're somewhere in the Pacific Ocean, south of Alaska and west of Canada. When I picture that place on a map in my mind, all I remember is a vast and empty ocean.

As we walk, I listen carefully for the sound of running water. My feet are bare. Effie's, too. She was wearing socks when the ship was wrecked, but she left them back with the others—I think right on Rosalind's feet. The ground beneath us is soft and wet, giving a bit beneath us as we walk, helping our footsteps stay quiet. Everything is covered in springy moss. Ferns grow in abundance. It is vibrant with life: bright flashes of purple flowers in places where the sun has penetrated the canopy, and bright blue fungus creeping up the trunks of the trees. It is lush, thriving, like the forest itself is the living thing.

The wound on my shoulder starts to ache terribly.

I keep shifting my arm to try to escape the pain.

"It's so strange here," I say, needing to talk. Eager for a distraction from the pain.

"It reminds me of a place back home, actually," Effie says.

"Really? It's nothing at all like Southern California."

"There's this forest near my granda's house, out in the country. He used to say the place was older than the kingdom itself, where the fae used to live." Effie laughs. "Granda always liked telling tales, especially when we were gullible little girls."

"What was it called?" I ask. "The ancient forest."

"I don't remember its map name. Granda just called it the Dark Wood. Told us not to go in there without him, or we'd get gobbled up by the 'fair folk,' as he called them. I loved his stories. He used to write plays for us," Effie says. "That's how it all started—with acting, I mean. Just putting on little shows for our family in the living room, wearing Nan's fancy old hats. I always did whatever it took to make them laugh, and Miri could always make them cry."

I smile at the warmth in Effie's voice talking about them. Then I wonder if she'll ever see home again.

"Look," Effie says, her voice hushed.

She gestures to a tree covered with twining vines, and a rusted red mark on the side of one. She places her hand over the stain, lining up her fingers.

It's a bloody handprint.

She pulls her hand away and rubs it on her pants, as though it's clung to her fingers, even though it's been long dry. As though she can wipe away the feeling of uncovering evidence you didn't want to see.

"Do you want to go back?" I ask. But my voice is raw, and I can't hide that from her. We really need to find water.

"No."

Effie's voice doesn't waver, and it's not my job to question her, so we forge on. There is nothing else for so long that a tendril of hope grows inside of me that there won't be any additional grim discoveries on our walk. I try to pay attention to the flora and fauna—there are bright blue mushrooms on nearly everything. They grow in clusters along fallen trees and the mossy areas of ground.

There are a few patches of berries, too; red and indigo, growing on bushes. I'm sure Everly would know if any of them are edible, but I have no idea. I pluck one from a bush and roll it between my fingers. It's so plump that with only the slightest pressure from my fingers, it bursts in my palm, a splash of red. My stomach cramps with hunger, and my throat has been parched for hours, and I want so badly to lick the juice from my fingers.

A hand like a vise on my arm makes me stop walking and look up. The berry slides slowly off my palm and plops onto the ground at my feet.

There is a tree just ahead of us, even wider than the others.

It is covered as high as I can see in blue mushrooms, though the ones at the bottom shimmer a slick violet color where they've been covered by crimson droplets.

Partway up the trunk, pinned right at eye level, is a curved line, like a snake coiled against the furrowed bark. For a moment, I think that's what it is: a snakeskin. But when I look closer, I realize that what I thought was a scaled pattern is in fact gaps of darkness between bones.

They are vertebrae, stacked on top of each other, blood-stained white against the moss-covered tree. It is a spine, curving upward. At the top, like a bloody, terrible crown, is a human skull.

ACT II

After Me Comes the Flood

Be not afeard; the isle is full of noises.

—*The Tempest*, Act III, Scene II

The skull is mostly bone. Only a few tender bits of muscle still cling to it.

The spine is pinned in place against the trunk. On either side of it are a set of ribs, splayed wide. There are chunks of flesh still attached to them, and that's where the blood is falling from in a steady, metronomic drip.

As we stand there, a bit of bloody tissue sloughs off a rib with a wet sound, sliding off the bone and falling at our feet on the forest floor.

"What in the hell," I whisper.

"Is that . . . it's him. It's Vincent."

"No," I say automatically, but I know it's a lie in the same moment that I say it. Something shines on the ground beneath the tree, and I reach for it, holding it up for a better look.

It's Vincent's cigar cutter.

"I don't understand," Effie says. "What could do this?"

She doesn't ask *who*. She asks what. But nothing I know

of could do this. It is unlike anything I've ever even heard of.

"A bear," I offer. I try to sound sure of myself, but Effie is already shaking her head at me. She knows as well as I do that no normal predator did this to Vincent.

"Do you think someone is here on the island with us?" she asks.

"It didn't sound like it, last night. There were . . . growls? And those screeches? It sounded like an animal, not a person. I thought it was a bear, or a pack of wolves."

"I heard them, too. But this is . . ." Effie trails off.

It's grisly, is what it is. Like something from a nightmare.

I take one last long look at the bones on the tree and step a bit closer. They're pinned in place—held there by little shards of white. I realize it's more bone—tiny, broken pieces, stabbed into the trunk of the tree to hold the spine and ribs in place. In my head I picture something standing here, taking the time to display the long length of spine and hold it in place.

Only hands would have the dexterity to do it.

"We should go." I place my hand on Effie's wrist, gentle but firm. She shouldn't be looking at this in the first place, and I don't want to stay here. I don't want to find out what did this.

"Effie, we promised the others we'd find water."

The reminder snaps Effie out of the fog, and she turns to me, her dark eyes bright with unshed tears. I'm not sure if she's mourning him or if she's just scared as hell, like I am. She tucks her red hair behind her ears and tilts her chin up slightly, so she's looking down her pretty nose at me.

"You're right. Let's go."

Effie and I turn and walk past the tree—I want badly to return to the others, but I crinkle the empty plastic bottle in my hand. I try to swallow against the rawness of my throat, but it's useless.

We break out of the denser part of the forest, and there's a small meadow.

A small fox streaks away as soon as we step out of the shadow of the trees. He is rust red with streaks of black down his sides. A rabbit takes off, too, and another small brown mammal. I can't think of the name for it. It is round and low like a groundhog.

"We should try to set some kind of traps out here," Effie says.

"That's a good idea."

"Did your sister teach you to make any kind of snare?"

I shake my head. "No, sorry."

"It's okay. We're smart. We'll figure it out."

"Do you really want to eat the little bunnies?" I ask.

"Right now? No. But I have a feeling that eventually I really will."

We cross the meadow, and I feel like I need to acknowledge what we saw on the tree. It was horrible for me, and I barely knew the man. I can't imagine what it was like for Effie.

"I'm sorry, Effie," I say. "He didn't deserve . . . whatever that was."

Effie stops walking and looks up at the sky. It's a clear summer day. Blue skies. Some kind of bird of prey swoops high overhead. A hawk, or perhaps even an eagle. It's jarring that the horror we just witnessed in the forest can coexist with the beauty we find out here, only yards away.

"Do you want to know how it started?" she asks.

She means Vincent.

"Only if you want to tell me."

"We filmed a television pilot together—it never aired. The project was canceled. But before it was, Vincent was really kind to me and Miri on set. It was my first real acting gig. He'd come by my trailer to rehearse lines with me. No one said anything, and I thought that was just how things were done. I was so flattered the first time he told me I was beautiful. And when he told me I was talented. When he said to never let them dye my hair. When he asked me if he could kiss me. '*Just once,*' he said. . . .

"That was three years ago," she added.

"Wait, so you were—"

"Not quite fifteen," Effie says. "In the pilot we were filming, he was playing my father."

I haven't eaten in a while, so when my stomach turns, I taste only bile in my throat. Effie had been a kid. There was nearly a thirty-year age gap between them.

"Effie," I start, then falter. I have no idea what to say to comfort that kind of hurt.

Her eyes are bright with unshed tears when they find mine. "I'm not grieving him, Liv. I'm relieved." She watches me closely, waiting for a condemnation. It isn't loss causing Effie pain right now, but guilt.

"It's okay, Effie. You don't have to explain to me. I get it."

"Thank you," she says. "Please, don't tell the others I told you that."

"I wouldn't," I offer, but I recognize the look in Effie's wide brown eyes. She doesn't know me well enough to trust me.

I was wrong about her. I thought Effie was aloof—cold, even. I thought she was conceited, and that's why she stayed apart from the rest of us.

But it was all because of him.

"Wait." I reach out and take Effie's hand in mine.

This is stupid.

I shouldn't be telling her this.

"I'm not supposed to be here."

Effie looks confused. "Right, well, none of us are supposed to be here, Liv."

"No, I don't mean the island. I mean the yacht. The internship. All of it. I . . . I cheated, Effie."

"What? How?"

"I stole my sister's information to apply. Her transcripts,

her extracurriculars, her impeccable grades, her clean record, even her name. I'm Violet Whitlock, not Everly. I forged the entire application, except for the writing section."

"Why?" Effie asks.

"I needed a way out, and I've gotten in trouble before. My name wasn't going to carry me very far."

"What kind of trouble?" Effie asks. I keep waiting for some thread of judgment to enter her voice, but she mostly just sounds curious.

"Um, I set a house on fire once, with an entire family inside, including me and my sister. And I got arrested for assault."

"Assault?"

"I hit my foster brother. Broke his nose."

"For real life? How old were you?" Effie asks, raising her eyebrows at me.

"Twelve," I tell her. "He was sixteen."

"Why did you do it?"

"Because he deserved it," I answer. I know Effie expected more of an explanation than that, and I'm grateful when she doesn't press for one.

"Honestly, that's impressive, Liv. You are still Liv, right?"

"Yes. Liv is really my nickname."

"No, I wasn't asking. I was telling you. *You're still Liv.* Right? You're you. Why would any of us care about what your grade point average was or if you punched some arsehole?

I actually might like you a little better for it."

"I—I'm just not a very good person. I'm a thief. And a liar, when it suits me."

"Liv, I've just finished telling you that I'm glad my boyfriend was butchered by some creature in the most violent way imaginable, after a night spent listening to him scream my name, begging for help. If you're a bad person, you're in good company. Besides, this feels like punishment enough, being stranded here.

"But thank you," she adds. "For the secret. I won't tell."

"Um, sure," I say, confused by the direction of this conversation. I don't know what I'd been expecting. All the things that mattered so much a day and a half ago suddenly . . . don't matter anymore. I rub my arms as though I'm trying to warm up. In truth, I'm feeling vulnerable, not cold. I'm not used to this. Letting my guard down and being accepted for who I am.

Effie made it easier by going first.

"I don't think we should be too scared of whatever it is out here," Effie says.

"You don't? Why the hell not?" I ask.

"It's some kind of monster. Maybe it's a man, and maybe it's a beast," she says. Then she shrugs that off, like the difference doesn't matter. "But we're teenage girls. We've all been prey before."

We are nearly across the meadow when I hear it. It's

little more than a rush of white noise from here, but it's the sound I've had my ears attuned to for every step of our trek through these woods.

"Water." I take off running with Effie close on my heels. There's less soft moss on the ground here, and I ignore prickles of sticks and stems and the rough catch of an occasional rock as I hurry across the meadow. We crash through the foliage on the other side, and there it is.

A wide creek winds its way through the mossy earth of the forest. It slips across smooth ovals of stone, clear and shining.

Effie sinks to her knees and cups the water in her palms.

"Wait!" I shout at her, reaching down to stop her hands before they touch her lips. "We have to boil it first, Effie. It could have anything living in it."

"But I'm so thirsty, Liv."

"I know. Me too." My throat burns with every swallow. "But we can't."

Effie doesn't drop the water in her hands but washes her face with it instead. She scoops up more and drips it over the back of her neck, cooling off her burning skin. She's already turned a bit pink from the sun.

I follow her lead, washing some of the grime and dried salt water and sweat from my body, as well as I can in the shallow water.

It isn't the relief we need most, but it helps.

"Look," Effie says.

Midway across, the water is deeper, and I see what Effie is pointing at. A silver flash of rainbow scales. There are fish here, too. We just need a way to catch them.

I fill up the four empty water bottles we brought from the beach. They aren't large, and we'll lose some of the volume when we boil it.

We'll have to find a better way to transport and hold water.

"We need to get out to the yacht." I'm thinking about how much could be in the waves just off the shoreline. It won't be there forever. The currents could pull the entire wreck away from land at any time.

Effie nods, quiet and thoughtful beside me as we start to make our way back. We cross the meadow and then change direction ever so slightly, giving the tree with Vincent's remains a wide berth. Seeing it once was enough.

"Rosa is a good swimmer," Effie says. "I'm sure she'll volunteer to try to get out to the wreck and see what can be saved."

The forest warms as we walk. It must be near noon, and I'm no longer freezing in the thin clothes I'm wearing.

"We shouldn't tell them what we found. I mean, not everything." Effie's eyes are fixed straight ahead, and even when I'm sure she knows I'm studying her, she won't look at me.

"Effie, we have to. They need to know what we're dealing with."

"Do we know what we're dealing with?" she asks.

"No, but—"

"We can tell them we know he's dead. That we found blood. A lot of it."

"Effie, I don't want to lie."

"Why stop now, *Violet*?" she says, meanness suddenly crowding her words.

"Effie." I've stopped walking, taken aback by her change. "I told Miri I wouldn't."

"Oh my god, that didn't take long," she says.

"What didn't?"

"Don't be thick. You like her. People will do anything for Miri. The golden child."

It's the last thing she says that keeps me from being mean right back to her, even as I feel my own spiteful words fill my mouth. There is heat creeping up my neck, first from anger, and then it's quickly replaced by shame. *The golden child*. I know what it's like to always be the second sister—in love, affection, praise. Effie Knight was being bitter.

Finally, I could genuinely relate to one of these girls.

"Effie, it's up to you. If you don't want to tell them exactly what we saw, we won't."

Effie turns on me, and I can see I've surprised her. "What?"

"He was your . . . whatever. You get to choose."

"Thank you," she says. She's clearly unused to getting her way. "We'll make sure they know that some kind of large animal likely did it, so they need to be careful and stay out of the forest."

"I'm sure that's enough. No one is ready to go gallivanting off on their own at this point."

"Right. You're right."

We reach the shore a few minutes later and are greeted with hugs and exclamations of joy over the water. Our news about Vincent sobers everyone.

"Are you sure he's dead?" Celia asks. "He could be badly hurt somewhere."

"He's dead." I say it with conviction, so Effie doesn't have to.

Celia and Miri exchange a look. They must have known all along about Effie and Vincent. Miri doesn't say anything else, but she does step forward and slip her hand into her sister's.

Celia takes the water bottles we filled at the creek and sets them apart from the sealed ones that washed ashore from the wreck.

"You didn't drink that water, did you?" Celia asks me and Effie.

I shake my head.

"Good," Celia says, relieved. "I forgot to remind you of that before you went off."

"It looks clean," Rosa says, lifting one of the bottles to the light.

"It's the microscopic friends we have to worry about," Celia explains. "Cryptosporidium. Giardia. Nematodes."

"In English, Celia," Paris says.

"Bacteria. Roundworms. Tiny little critters that can kill

us just as well as starvation or thirst or exposure."

"Gross," Miri says. She holds the water bottles at arm's length in front of her.

"They can't fly, Miri." Celia takes the bottles from her.

Exposure. That's the next thing. We could go a few days without food, but none of us wants to be in the woods at night.

"We need shelter. We need it before dark. We can't sleep on the rocks again."

"Here. Come with me." Miri grabs for my hand. "We were busy while you two were gone."

She drags me up the beach, closer to the place where Rosa and I washed up. I can still see the wreck out in the waves, caught on the rocky shore, pieces of broken metal and hull jutting out of the water.

But the real bounty is already onshore.

"Ta-da," Miri sings, gesturing to the small mountain of supplies they've gathered.

They've piled it high. There are cushions from the seating on deck and in the cockpit. They are wide and covered in waterproof material that will hold up well out here. I'm silently grateful that Vincent Bellegarde appreciated the finer touches on his yacht. There are about a dozen more water bottles and Coke cans, and something shining with silver metal. It's a teakettle. It's dented in a few spots, but it'll hold. If we build another fire, we can boil water.

The last thing that's washed up is a large piece of fabric, maybe ten feet long and half as wide. If we can find a good place for it, we should be able to make a tentlike shelter out of it. It takes me a second to recognize it as belonging to one of the sofas from our living area—they had these leather covers over them. That space must have been torn to shreds on the rocks. It could have so easily been our bodies instead, smashed and scraped against them.

But the image that flashes in my head isn't of myself as a bloody, pulpy mess on the rocks, but of the spine and ribs in the woods. The skin and muscle left clinging to bone.

My stomach growls with hunger.

Miri either hears my stomach or reads my mind.

"Hungry? Did anything look promising out there?" She nods toward the trees looming beside us as the others walk up the beach to join us.

"Nothing obvious," I tell her. "Lots of berries, but I don't know what is edible. Animals we don't know how to catch."

"Fish in the creek we found," Effie adds. "That we also don't know how to catch."

"There was so much food on that damn ship," Celia says. "Most of it perishable. Fresh caviar, but no cans of tuna."

"There were granola bars," Rosa says.

"And protein shakes, in that mini-fridge by the sofa," Paris adds.

"Then those are the goal today. We can always try again later for other items," I say.

"There's no guarantee anything is still out there—it could all be miles out to sea," Effie says from where she'd been quietly stacking the chair cushions.

"We have to try," Miri says. "Who can swim? Like, *really* swim."

"Me." Rosa steps forward. She's still pale but looks a hundred times better than yesterday. She's been drinking water consistently. Before any of us can object, she starts stretching her arms to prep for the swim.

"And me," Miri says. "I can do it."

We all look out at the water. It doesn't look as rough now that the storm has fully passed.

Nor does it look easy or inviting.

"Rosa, you need to look for Vincent's emergency satellite phone. It's stored in a case, and thank god for that, because it's waterproof. Vincent only buying the best available might save our life. The box will be a bright color, neon green or yellow. I know he had one. I saw it once."

"I thought it was all broken," I say.

"Not this," Celia says. "It wouldn't have been connected to the yacht in any way. It's like a personal locator GPS. It's our best chance of getting off this island if we can activate it."

"Then why didn't Vincent use it? During the storm?"

"He panicked," Effie says. "He probably forgot it even existed. He liked to play at captain, but he wasn't, he couldn't . . ."

"Green box. Got it," Rosa says. "Well, there's no point in waiting. I'll just talk myself out of it."

She's already pulling off the blanket we've had her wrapped in for the past day to keep her warm. She strips out of her jeans, too. They'll be too heavy in the water. It feels like we are about to undo all our hard work to keep Rosa alive.

Miri returns my sweatshirt to me. When I pull it over my head, I can smell her on the inside of it—sweat and ocean and a hint of citrus and something else that's simply her. Once it's on, I feel the warmth of her body heat still clinging to the soft inner fleece.

Miri and Rosa wade into the water. The waves are constant, but not high or very strong. It's the rip currents that will matter the most, but I have to believe that if there was a strong one this close to shore, there wouldn't be much left of the yacht in the shallows around the island.

The girls dive under the waves, surfacing occasionally to breathe, swimming hard and fast for the ship remains.

The rest of us have things we could be doing—should be doing. Going back into the forest to fill more water bottles. Starting to fashion a shelter to sleep in tonight. But we are frozen on the sand and rocks, hands pressed to our foreheads to block the glare of sunlight on water.

Rosa reaches the yacht first. I can make out her dark hair against the white helm where the *N-C-A* of the yacht's name are sticking out of the water. She signals for Miri to stay there, and dives underwater.

It must be only a minute, but it feels much longer as we

wait, watching the choppy surface of the ocean where Rosa disappeared. Miri looks back at us. She is easy to spot, her blond hair bright against the gray-green water.

Something bobs up to the surface, and Miri grabs it, holds it up triumphantly, and waves it at us.

"I think it's a can of something," Celia says. Paris stands just behind her, arms wrapped around Celia, head tucked over Celia's shoulder. We all lean forward, unable to help ourselves, as though seeing something edible would be almost as good as consuming it. Like just the promise of it could be enough.

More bottles float up beside Miri, and she swims around, gathering them. Finally, Rosa breaks the surface, gasping for air. She passes something larger to Miri and goes under again.

They're out there for fifteen minutes, maybe less. Every few minutes, I step forward, ready to go in after them at the first sign of trouble, until eventually my legs are knee-deep in the waves. I ignore the crabs scurrying across my feet.

When they start to swim back, I can't help myself. I peel off my sweatshirt and throw it to Effie onshore. I swim until I'm past the first break of waves.

I reach Miri first. Rosa is struggling to keep up behind her.

Miri has a strap across her shoulder, and it takes me a second to recognize my own faded purple backpack. It's soaked through and filled with the bottles they collected from the ship, weighing Miri down.

"I'm okay," she says. "Get her."

I swim out to Rosa.

"She's dead. The chef, Ms. Simmons," Rosa says when I reach her. I ought to ask her what she saw, or if she's okay, but I'm selfish. I don't want another image of a dead body in my mind.

"Is that food?" I ask instead. She found granola bars—an entire box of them, but it's falling to pieces as she swims, and she's struggling to keep all the bars inside. Once I take the waterlogged cardboard from her hands, Rosa begins to swim in earnest. I clutch the precious cargo against my chest and swim back with my one free arm. Onshore, Miri and Rosa lie out like starfish on the sand, breathing heavily. Their clothes cling to their bodies, and I turn away, giving them some privacy while they recover.

"Here." I open my backpack and pull out the protein shakes, handing them out. There are a dozen, so two for each of us. None of us can wait a second longer, and we each drink one entire can down.

"The emergency locator?" Celia asks after draining hers empty.

I shake my head.

"There's nothing else here," I say.

"I didn't see it, Celia. I'm sorry. I'll try again." Rosa's breathing has finally returned to normal, and she moves to sit beside me in the sand. There is dirt smeared across her face, but when I reach out to wipe it off, it is slick.

"Rosa, are you bleeding?"

I hold out my hand to show her the streak of bright red across my fingertips. Rosa wipes her cheek, and the blood comes off. She checks her arms.

"Rosa," Paris says. "It's your foot."

Rosa sits back and stretches out her feet. Her right foot is covered in sand and blood.

Her smallest toe is dangling off the side of it. It is barely still attached, holding on by just a small bit of skin and muscle. There is a hint of white bone visible in her foot where the toe was meant to be.

"Excuse me," Miri says, and rushes from the group. Celia chases after her, and a moment later I can hear the sound of retching from the rocks behind us.

There's a not-small part of me that wants to run, too. To pretend this isn't real. The protein shake sloshes around in my stomach, riotous. I gulp against the feeling and breathe slowly in and out. I know Miri couldn't help it, but the thought comes to me anyway.

It's such a waste of food.

I turn my attention back to Rosa, anticipating her own horror at the injury. Instead, I find her smiling. Somehow that is worse.

"Rosa?" I take her chin in my fingers and turn her face

to mine, noting the sparkle of amusement in her big brown eyes. "Rosa, are you all right?"

"It's just the funniest thing," she says. "I can't feel it at all."

"Your extremities are numb from the water. You must have kicked a sharp metal edge on the boat or something."

She giggles. "If you say so."

I think she's in shock.

We shouldn't have let her go out there. She'd barely recovered from the wreck. So stupid. I should have taken better care of her.

I start to dig through the contents of my backpack. Ruined notebooks and ballpoint pens. I try not to get distracted by the joy I feel when I find my sneakers. I forgot they were in there. There's also a jar of peanut butter and a packet of saltines. I'd thrown them in before I got on my bus so that I'd have dinner during the long ride, but I'd slept instead and never opened them.

But none of these things are what I need.

I unzip the front pocket and find it. A first aid kit.

It might be the only piece of advice I'd taken from Everly—to keep one in my bag. Just in case. Inside the tin is an assortment of bandages and wraps, and I reach for a small roll of gauze and the sewing kit. Everything is wet, but the gauze was wrapped in plastic, so at least that is usable now.

"Effie, do you have the lighter? And then we need a fire,

like, as fast as you can."

Effie starts to gather items that can be kindling. The pages from my notebooks are too wet. She and Paris hurry to the woods for some leaves and branches, and when they return Effie does the same thing I did the night before, ripping a strip of cloth from the hem of her pajama pants to help start the fire.

"Hey, Rosa?" I say, laying out the items I need. "I'm not going to lie to you, this is going feel pretty bad as soon as you start feeling your foot again."

"I've got a high pain tolerance."

"Are you sure?" I ask.

"Last summer I finished my floor routine with a broken ankle."

"Do you mean when you won all those medals?"

Rosa nods. "Yep. Performing on the injury ended my career. But trust me, I can handle the pain, Liv. Promise. Just fix it."

I shake my head but keep moving, preparing for what I know I need to do. It's not like there is much choice here. Either I try to stitch her up, or she loses the toe. I heat the smallest needle from the sewing kit in the lighter flame to sterilize it as best I can. Effie and Paris have the fire started, so I empty one of the water bottles we brought back from the creek into the teakettle and set it onto the flames.

"When it's boiling, strip some cloth from the blanket or

whatever washed onshore. We ought to wrap up her foot as well as we can when I'm done."

Paris perches beside Rosa and takes her hand.

I thread the needle and examine Rosa's foot. As gently as I can, I push the dangling toe back into place.

"Hey, so tell me how you fell in with the starlets," I tell her.

"I know what you're doing, and you don't have to," Rosa says. "I'm used to pain."

"Well, I'm not used to sewing toes on, so maybe I need the distraction."

Rosa smiles. "Fine, but don't sew it on sideways or something because you aren't paying attention."

I pinch the needle tight and begin. Rosa flinches once, and then holds still.

"I met Paris at some fancy LA party, what, two years ago?"

Paris nods. "It was one of Vincent's, actually."

"That's right," Rosa says. She laughs and then sucks in air sharply when the needle pierces her flesh again. "I was out there meeting with publicists, working on endorsements. Weirdly enough, Paris and I had a lot in common."

"How so?" I ask. I'm nearly done.

"I guess just being known for one particular thing. Idolized for it. Paris had her voice, I had my sport. But we both felt pretty invisible except for those parts of us."

"You asked me how I'd feel if I lost it all overnight," Paris recalls.

"And you said you think you'd be relieved," Rosa says.

"To be clear, this isn't exactly what I had in mind during that conversation," Paris says.

Rosa's laugh is shallow, her grip on Paris so tight that both rows of their knuckles are stark white. I manage a few final stitches—three on the top of her foot and three on the bottom. The angle is too awkward, and my fingers too slick with blood, to manage any more than that. It would help if I had any idea what I was doing.

A piercing sound interrupts the quiet as I'm tying knots into the thin black thread. It's the teakettle, whistling despite its bumps and bruises.

Once Rosa's foot is stitched and wrapped in gauze, I wind the clean strips of cloth around it. I'm not sure how tight to make it—I don't want to cut off circulation, but it needs to be protected from infection. No one else knows, either, so I do the best I can.

Finally, I sit back on my heels, admiring my rough, but serviceable, handiwork.

"Why did we even have a teakettle on board?" I wonder out loud.

"I brought it," Effie says. "We weren't about to rely on you Americans and your absurd notions of how to make tea. The kettle was our great-nan's. Survived the war."

"And now a damned shipwreck," Miri adds. She and Celia had stayed a distance away while I worked on Rosa's foot—for the better, so I could focus without worrying about Miri passing out over the blood or throwing up again.

I leave Rosa in the care of Effie. She's curled up now, her head on Effie's lap by the fire. She isn't sleeping, but her eyes are closed. I hope she can rest, despite the pain she must be in. I find the first aid kit again and pour out two pain reliever pills for Rosa. I turn the small capsule in my hand, counting how many are left inside. Sixteen. That'll only last her a few days.

I rinse the blood off my hands in the ocean. My shoulder is throbbing now, and itches like hell on top of that, so I sink down to my knees and let the frigid water wash over my upper body, soothing the hurt. My clothes turn practically translucent, but honestly, without Vincent here, I can't bring myself to care.

When I walk back to the others, Celia and Paris have started to boil the water from the creek again. It's time-consuming with such a small kettle, but necessary.

"Want to try to build a shelter with me?" I ask Miri.

"Sure," she says.

We walk up the beach to the pile of items they gathered from the beach, and I start to sort through them. "What the hell is this?"

I lift a soggy mass of . . . hair?

"It's a wig, I think," Miri says. "The cargo had set items, remember?"

Miri flips it over and shows me the inner netting holding it in place.

"Maybe it will burn?" I wonder. I'm trying to think of how we can use it.

"If it's synthetic, it'll just melt, right?" Miri says.

I shrug. I haven't the slightest idea.

We still have the seat cushions, and a wide plank of wood—I think the lid of a crate.

"Wait, I have an idea," I tell Miri.

I try to lift the wood, but as soon as I put weight on it, pain laces up my bad arm and I cry out. Before I can ask, Miri is there, lifting the board for me.

"Where?" she asks.

There is a group of rocks farther back from the water—not quite under the forest's canopy, but at the edge of it. Two large rocks face each other with a hollowed-out space in between them. I explain my idea to Miri, and together we lift the board up on top of the rocks. My arm screams in protest, but we get it done. It lies flat, creating a kind of rough roof overhead.

When we are done, it's somewhat like a cave. The rocks meet at the back, which will shield us from the forest. We pull the sofa cover over the board and weigh it down with rocks in the sand. The cover is made of leather, so I think it will hold up against the weather for a while, at least. We line the inside of our rocky cave with the seat cushions and lay the blanket over top. It will be cramped with all of us inside, but that means we'll be warm at night.

At night, when a killer roams the island. The sun has started to set, and I feel a chill creeping up my spine at the idea of facing another night on this island.

"Well?" Miri asks, hands on her hips as she surveys our work. "What do you think?"

"Honestly? We nailed it. It's practically cottage-core," I say.

Miri walks back over to the pile of items left on the beach.

"Oh my god!" she shouts.

"What? What's wrong?" I jog over to her, ignoring how the bouncing feels like little jolts of lightning up my arm.

"Champagne," Miri says, lifting a sealed bottle from the sand.

"Miri. Don't shout like that! You scared the hell out of me, and don't—"

I'm too late. She's popped the cork, and champagne bubbles up over the lip of the bottle, spilling onto the sand.

"Miri, what the hell. We can't waste anything."

"I'm not wasting it, Liv." Miri licks champagne off the tips of her fingers. "I'm enjoying it. But please, enlighten me. How will a single bottle of champagne save us in this place?"

"You're being a brat again," I tell her.

"Thank you for your honesty," she says, and puts the bottle to her lips, drinking it down.

I reach out, grabbing the bottle from her hands. "God, Miri, one second you're throwing up at the sight of blood—"

"You mean Rosa's severed toe," Miri chimes in, raising her eyebrows at me.

"And the next second you are actually helping me with shelter, and I'm thinking, *Wow, maybe I underestimated her,* and then you do this!"

"I'm happy to share the champagne, if that's what's got your knickers twisted."

I'm too angry to answer, so I don't.

"Where the hell are you going?" she calls as I stomp into the forest.

"We need wood for the fire, Miri. I'm going to find a way to be useful. Enjoy your drink."

She calls after me again, but I ignore her. It isn't until I'm about a dozen or so yards into the forest that I stop. It's much darker than I thought it would be, night already falling under the canopy where sunlight can hardly penetrate it even at the brightest parts of the day.

I turn back the way I came, but as I walk, it only gets darker around me. *Shit.* I try another direction, expecting to fall out of the trees and onto the beach at any moment. There's only moss and pines and thick ferns.

"Miri!" I call out. "Miri? I got turned around! Where are you?"

There's no answer.

I stop walking for a moment to get my bearings, sitting on a toppled rotting tree. My arm is nearly unbearable now.

I need to take the bandage off, but I already know what I'll find there. When I hold my arm, the scars on it are bright white circles on skin that is hot and swollen and red. It's infected.

I get up again and start to walk, slower this time, listening for the sounds of the others or the waves on the shore, but my head aches. I keep thinking I hear the ocean, when it's just the roar of blood pounding in my ears.

There's something strange about the moss I'm walking on. Dark green patches align with lighter ones, back and forth. It's forming a pattern, like a checkerboard. I shake my head. That doesn't make any sense.

But when I look up again, I'm in a room. It's a kitchen, and it's familiar to me in a way, though now it's made entirely out of parts of the forest. The table is carved from the trunk of a pine. The window is twisted out of branches, with vines hanging down as curtains. And there, on the table, a bowl of shining red apples. Then someone reaches for an apple, and the arm is so thin, and so small. It belongs to a child. A little girl.

I watch my sister sink her teeth into the fresh fruit. I know she's hungry, but we aren't supposed to eat without permission. She broke the rules, and she'll be punished.

I snatch the apple from her and tell her to hide. A shadow moves over me, and a massive hand seizes my wrist. This time, I know what's coming, and I try to pull away. A glowing red ember falls on me, burning my skin in a perfect circle, and then another, and one more. Right up my arm in a line.

It's the last time, I tell myself. I'm getting us out of here, before she gets hurt. But instead of burning curtains, I am burning vines. I smell the sweetness of the fruit in my hand, and the salt of the ocean. I smell the acrid scent of cigarettes and burned flesh.

Sweetness coats my tongue.

I'm standing in the forest, holding a piece of fruit in my hands that I'm not sure I recognize. It's definitely not the apple I'd imagined it to be.

But the juice is tart, an ambrosia that floods my whole mouth, and a soft cry of genuine joy escapes me. I don't really care if it kills me. I want to eat them until I burst. At least I'd die with a belly full and my thirst truly sated for the first time in days.

The inside of the fruit is dark pink, fleshy, and seeded. I think it's a fig of some kind.

"Liv!" A crashing sound to my right, and Miri breaks through the forest, stopping dead in her tracks at the sight of me. "What the hell, Liv. I've been calling you."

"I got lost," I tell her.

"The beach is just through there," she says. "Why didn't you call out?"

"I did," I start to tell her, but I can't explain it. I don't know what happened to me.

"Did you eat that?" she asks, noticing the fruit in my hand. "It could be poisonous."

"I guess we'll find out," I say.

Miri takes my good arm and leads me back to the beach, where the others have gathered, looking concerned.

Effie and Celia help move Rosa to our makeshift shelter, and I lean against one of the rocks, away from the others, watching Paris start a new fire. We have strips of dry cloth now, and she uses one of those as tinder.

I can't help it, my eyes keep going to the dark edge of the woods, trying to make sense of what I saw in there. It was like a memory and a nightmare all in one.

Probably just a hallucination. I'm feverish from my arm, and so dehydrated.

Effie joins me a few minutes later.

"We should take turns watching the forest," she says, her voice low. "If the others think it's a wolf or a bear, they won't expect it to come back."

"But we do?" I ask pointedly. I'm exhausted, and I still think we should have told the others everything.

"I don't know," Effie says. "But we agreed—"

"You dictated, Effie. That's not an agreement."

"Do you think scaring them will really help right now?" Her voice is strained, almost panicked.

"Okay, Effie. It's fine. We'll take turns on watch tonight," I reassure her. "And let the others get some real rest."

I leave Effie and go find my backpack. The ocean water evaporated off it in the sun, leaving streaks of white salty residue on the faded purple canvas. We pass around protein bars, eating them quickly—ravenously.

But they aren't the real surprise.

Next, I pull out the crackers and peanut butter, and when she sees them, Celia gasps.

"Liv. Seriously. Are you an angel? I think you're an angel," she says, leaning forward.

I sink down to the sand around the fire and let Rosa rest her head on my thigh. She smiles up at me, even though I'm sure her foot must be hurting like hell. A couple of ibuprofen are no match for her mangled toe.

We each take two crackers and scoop out peanut butter, sandwiching it between them. Without discussing the plan, we all eat slowly this time. We savor every single lick. Every crumb of the cracker until it's gone.

We aren't exactly full after our meal, but it's the first real food in our stomachs in two days, and it's satisfying enough to lift our moods. Especially when we can follow the dry meal with the fresh water that Celia and Paris spent the evening boiling clean.

I keep my attention split—half on the girls and the fire and the sweet comfort of food in my stomach—and the rest on the line of dark trees. Now that the sun has fully set, I'm aware of each sound in the forest, my senses heightened.

The truth is, I'm too exhausted to do more than just listen for anything that sounds wrong. We wouldn't have the energy to fight off a predator if it came for us tonight.

But for now, the birds are still fluttering in the trees, not quite settled for the night. There are insects chirping. The forest is alive—not the hushed, unnatural silence that came last night just before Vincent was attacked.

"I miss doom-scrolling," Paris says, her voice laden with sleepiness even though it's early. We haven't stopped moving since we woke up with the sun, and Miri and Rosa in particular spent more energy than they've consumed, with the swim out to the wreck.

We should have given them an extra scoop of peanut butter.

"Doom-scrolling?" Celia echoes with a soft laugh. "I get that. All the worries of the world, locked away behind a glowing screen. That sounds nice right now."

"Exactly," Paris says. "You get it."

"I miss hot water," Rosa says from where she's lying on my lap. She's got my sweatshirt on but she's shivering a bit, even right next to the fire. "I think I'd actually kill someone to get a hot shower right now, and some shampoo and conditioner."

Rosa's hair is matted from the swim in the ocean. While she lies there, I begin to comb it out gently with my fingers.

I figure sleep is the most important thing right now, but I want to check on her foot first thing in the morning. When my fingers brush against her forehead, it feels hot.

"I'd love some hand sanitizer," Miri says, holding her hands up to the firelight and examining her dirty nails. "I've been washing my hands all day in the ocean, and they're sticky. And I want a bag of crisps. I haven't eaten crisps since I was . . . I don't know, ten?"

I follow the lines of Miri's fingertips up her arm to her narrow shoulders. I notice just how thin she really is, and I remember the splash of a headline scrolling across my phone a few months ago. Rumors about Miri Knight and an eating disorder and a clinic. Tabloids acting like they weren't the cause of it.

We've all been prey before, Effie said in the woods. I think she must have meant Miri, too. I feel bad for yelling at her over the champagne. It will hardly be the difference between us dying or surviving here.

"I miss my bed," Celia says. "Though I've got to admit, you've done a good job with these cushions in here. Real cozy. And, of course, I miss Sir Ian."

"Sir Ian?" I ask.

"Her bulldog," Paris says. "We almost brought him."

"Thank the goddesses we didn't," Celia says. "He'd have sunk like a stone." She lifts a rock from the beach and drops it for emphasis.

"French bulldog?" I ask.

"Ach, I'm offended!" Celia laughs. "Sir Ian is a proper English gentleman, of course."

We all laugh, forgetting our hunger and our circumstances for a single, shining moment.

"What about you, Ef?" Miri asks. "What are you missing?"

"Books," Effie says without hesitation. "I haven't gone this long without reading since I learned how."

But we do have books. I had a few in my backpack with my notebooks. I'd laid them out earlier on top of our little shelter, to see if they'd dry out a bit.

"Hey, Paris, can you check the books up there?" I point them out so I don't have to ask Rosa to move. "Are any dry?"

"The notebooks are soggy pulp. I'm not sure there is much hope for them. Wait—the Shakespeare is mostly intact."

She brings it over and hands it to me. I flip through the book gently, its pages still quite damp. I'd brought it on a whim, figuring I ought to brush up on my knowledge if I was going to be on the set of an adaptation. It's a collection of plays and sonnets. Effie consults the table of contents. She's careful with the wet pages, slowly peeling them apart before turning to the page she wants and beginning to read.

"Be not afeard; the isle is full of noises,
Sounds and sweet airs, that give delight, and hurt not.
Sometimes a thousand twangling instruments

Will hum about mine ears; and sometime voices,
That, if I then had waked after long sleep,
Will make me sleep again: and then, in dreaming,
The clouds methought would open, and show riches
Ready to drop upon me; that, when I waked,
I cried to dream again."

Effie stops reading.

"I'm sorry," she says. "I've had bits and pieces of that stuck in my head all day."

"No," Rosa says. "It's all right. Keep reading."

Effie scans our faces and seems to find no objections, so she reads on.

I'm not sure when I drift to sleep. It's the calm surety of Effie's reading. She knows some of the passages by heart and adds gestures and breaks in the monologues. It's the low timbre of her voice, and her English accent, the crackling of our small fire, and the waves on the rocks.

One moment I am sitting there enthralled by Effie's easy delivery of *The Tempest*. The next I am jolted awake by a piercing scream.

It's Rosa.

She's risen from our little camp and is limping toward the ocean.

"Rosa, stop!" I shout. She'll ruin her bandages.

I reach Rosa before she gets to the water and all but tackle her to the sand. When my hands land on her skin, I pull back. She is burning up. I reach for her forehead and confirm that she's fevered. She cries out, and I realize I'm lying right across her injured foot. I shift back, but I don't release her leg.

"Get it off!" she starts screaming, tearing at the bandages around her foot.

I don't know what else to do—she is frantic, crying—so I help her, untying the knots I carefully put in place a few hours ago. My fingers brush on something cool and hard, and I pull back.

Clouds hide the moon, and there is no light this far away from the fire, so I can't see what is there, only a dark shadow across her skin.

Effie and Miri catch up with us, kneeling in the sand beside me. Rosa has stopped screaming, but there are little whimpers coming from her.

"Help me get her back up there," I say. We gently lift her, my concern growing when her head lolls onto my shoulder.

"She might pass out; keep a good grip on her," I tell them.

We make it back to the fire, where Paris and Celia are now awake, too, staring wide-eyed at us when we collapse beside the fire. It's died down, but it's still burning and giving off a glowing orange light. I shift Rosa's foot forward to get a better look.

My fingers trace what I felt in the dark before. Rosa is staring at her foot in a mixture of confusion and pain.

"It hurts," she whispers between clenched teeth.

Her entire foot is changed. It was inflamed before, sure, swollen from the injury and messy stitches. Now it is smooth, and sleek, and an iridescent green-blue color that shimmers in the firelight.

"Are those . . ." Effie begins but trails off, unable to say it.

"They're scales," Rosa says.

Her voice is as sharp as a serrated knife, severing us from our sleepy confusion. She's right. There's no confusion over *what* we are looking at. Even if it doesn't make any sense.

She wiggles her toes. The smallest one has a thin line where it had been detached, but that's the only remnant of her injury. When she spreads them apart, I reach out, catching them and showing her the thin, almost see-through film between them.

Rosa's toes are webbed.

I stay awake long after the others fall asleep.

None of them mean to. We take turns examining Rosa's foot and trying to guess what it could be. What it could mean. Our conclusion is that it is a strange infection, though I don't think a single one of us really believes that.

For hours after that it is a battle of wills—on one side, our bone-deep exhaustion, and on the other, our growing fear. But when the first red streaks of daylight stretch their fingers across the night sky, sleep has won for the others, and fear has won for me.

While Rosa sleeps, I watch as the purple-blue bruising on her ankle cracks, starts to bleed, and then hardens into new scales. I continue to check on it, but it seems to stop there, at her ankle. It doesn't spread to the unbruised skin of her leg.

I won't sleep again, so I get up and stretch my left arm. At this point, my injured right shoulder hurts too much to even shrug.

At least no monsters emerged to tear us to pieces and display our parts like wicked trophies on the trees. We survived a second night on our strange island.

I put my hand on my head and press hard on my temple, like that could clear the image of Vincent's spine from my brain, as though I'm wringing out a wet washcloth. It's a stupid gesture. A pointless one. The memory isn't going anywhere. I can't shake it, and I feel like we should have told the others exactly how we found Vincent. After what I saw in the woods yesterday—or imagined I saw—it feels like every secret I've ever kept is trying to claw its way out of me. Running away from a good home. Setting curtains on fire with the shaking hands of a child. Leaving out the details of a bloody spine pinned to a tree. So many half-truths, so many almost-lies.

I make my way up and down the shore to gather the few items that have washed up overnight from the wreck. I find a tin of baking soda, still sealed, and some kind of crumpled metal framework—I don't know what it could be from—maybe part of the ship? Or a kitchen appliance? But I have an idea, and hurry back to our little camp.

I reach for one of the wigs that washed up and flip it inside out. Sure enough, the inside has a structure webbing of material threaded back and forth. I use nail clippers from the first aid kit to detach the strands of hair from the net underneath.

My hurt arm refuses to cooperate, so it takes several tries to stretch the material over the metal framework. But when I manage it, I smile at the misshapen thing I've made.

"What's that?" Celia asks, sitting up from her place beside Paris in the shelter.

The space we made is long and narrow, stretching under the rocky outcropping, so we all had to lie close, almost on top of each other. It takes Celia a minute to extract herself without waking anyone.

"The creek we found had some fish in it," I say, and hold out my contraption.

"It's a net." Celia smiles at me. "Well done, Liv. When do you want to go try it out?"

"I can go now. Sun is up. There are animals moving around in the woods, so . . . so I think it's safe enough."

"I'm convinced. I'll come along," Celia says. She goes back to the shelter and wakes Paris to tell her where we're going. Paris leans up for a quick kiss goodbye, and I turn away. The moment is so soft and intimate, I feel like I'm intruding.

I put on my sneakers and wait for Celia at the edge of the forest, makeshift net in one hand and a few newly emptied water bottles in the other. When I try to swing my backpack onto my shoulders, I cry out. I drop the bag with a guttural sound. My shoulder can't hold it.

Celia comes up behind me, lifting the backpack without a word.

We stare into the forest a moment longer than necessary before we start to walk. The harsh crunching of branches under my sneakers throws me off. I've gotten used to the softness of bare feet, and I feel guilty for wearing shoes when Celia has none, though she doesn't complain.

We stop after a half hour when we find a bush with the same blue fruit I ate last night.

"Are these safe?" Celia asks as I pluck a few from the branches.

"Yeah, I'm pretty sure," I say. "I ate one yesterday, as a test." It feels easier to let her think I did it on purpose than to try to explain that I'm hallucinating things.

"You could have poisoned yourself, Liv. That's a pretty big risk to take," Celia says.

"We're going to starve if we don't try."

We eat the figs fast, so focused on consuming them that neither of us speak. We grin at the sweetness, and let the purple juice run down our chins.

They're still the best things I've ever tasted.

When I crouch lower to pick some more, I notice the blue mushrooms growing and decaying beneath the tree. They're the same violet-blue as the figs themselves. I pick one and smell it, and then smash it a bit between my fingers. I wonder if they're edible, too. They'd be a good source of protein.

Right now, it isn't worth the risk.

I brush the mushroom off my hands and rise. There is a

familiar patch of thin trees ahead—I recognize it from the day before with Effie.

"We should go around," I say, pointing off to the side. "We aren't far from where we found . . . the blood."

"Are you sure?" Celia asks, cocking her head to the side. "I can handle it."

"It's not a good idea," I tell her. I try to sound more nonchalant than I am. I brush away what feels like spiderwebs across my arms, only to realize it's goose bumps. I don't want to go back to that thicket with the tree and the bones.

"Fair enough," Celia agrees.

I wonder if I look as sick as I feel, and that's why she doesn't press the issue.

Once we reach the creek, I take off my sneakers and Celia and I step into the water and stretch the net between us. It is even colder than I remember.

There are plenty of fish. I think they might be salmon. They're huge. Just one would feed us all. But it takes Celia and me ten minutes to coordinate enough, and be fast enough, to swing the net up out of the water when a fish swims into it.

The first time it works, we are so surprised that we stand there and watch it flop off the net, back into the creek.

"Son of a bitch," I seethe.

"Once more," Celia says. "C'mon. We've got it sorted out now. We just have to hold on to it."

We swing the net again, trapping a new fish. This time Celia rushes forward, pressing our ends of the net together. The metal framework bends, flexible, but only to a point. We hurry out of the water, our numb feet slipping against the rocks.

We collapse on the embankment with the net above us.

Celia starts to laugh.

"That was so damn hard," she says. "We're for sure going to die out here if we don't get better."

I smile with Celia, but I can't laugh.

I'm too tired. My shoulder hurts too badly.

I turn my head to face her, not caring that my hair drags through the dirt. It's beyond hope already; a little dirt won't change much. Celia must agree, because her head is in dirt, too, with her arms stretched up above her and her braids splayed out beneath her. She has on the same tank top and pajama bottoms she's worn the last two days, though the maroon pants are soaked from the creek. Despite all of it—the dirt and the muddy clothes—Celia looks pretty with her lingering smile and the sunlight filtering through the trees to dance across her face.

"Tell me about you and Miri," I say. "You said you've been friends a while?"

"Right, yeah, for ages. We grew up on the same street. I think our mums were even in the same prenatal yoga classes or some shit."

"Destined to be friends."

"No, not exactly. We lost touch with each other when she and Effie left school and started spending more time on sets than home. But she reached out last Christmas. They were having a little party and invited me over. That's when I met Paris. I played piano and she sang carols."

"Love at first sight?" I tease.

"Sort of, yeah," Celia admits. "I mean, it helped that she's a goddess on earth when she sings. But when we started chatting it was, like, electric. I wanted to kiss her in the first five minutes. I was holding myself back from it all night."

"That's stupid cute," I tell her, crinkling my nose.

"I know," Celia says, drawing out the word, and covering her face with her hands in embarrassment. "So embarrassing, but it's true. I adored her. Instantly."

"What happened?"

"Yeah, well, I waited—to kiss her, I mean. She walked me home, and it started to snow. Then at my front gate, she was the one who kissed me."

"That sounds perfect."

"It was . . . incredible. It was actually my first kiss, like, ever. But my father saw. And he wasn't exactly keen on the idea of me dating a girl."

Celia phrases it in such simple terms, but I can hear the hurt in her voice.

"I'm sorry, Celia. What made him come around?" I ask.

"Nothing," she says. "I left for boarding school a week later, and I've spent most of my breaks with Paris instead of going home.

"I love her," Celia says. "I'm in love with her. I have been for a while, but it's terrifying out there. Not even my own parents accept it, and she thinks the world will? I don't know how she isn't scared."

"Well, we aren't out there now," I tell her. "You can love her here. No one will hurt you for it or make you afraid."

Celia smiles. "Finally, a silver lining."

We lie there a few minutes longer, letting the warm sunlight dance across our faces with our eyes closed. I feel content for the first time since our wreck. I feel like maybe we won't die here.

I stand up and reach for her with my good arm, grabbing her hands and pulling her to her feet. Celia puts her hands on her hips and looks down at the salmon we caught.

"How are we going to get that monster back to camp? It's so heavy."

"Well," I say, eyeing it up. "It'll be a lot lighter once we gut it."

The nail clippers are the best tool we have for the job. There is a little file inside that pivots out, and while it isn't sharp, it's pointed enough that I can hopefully stab it into the pale underside of the fish. As Celia flips it over, the rows of blue-green scales catch the light, creating rippling rainbows on Celia's brown skin while she holds it in place.

Celia is frowning.

"The scales are just like—"

"Please, *please* don't say it." I can't think about Rosa's foot and do this at the same time.

"Sorry," Celia says.

The first part isn't so bad. The stabbing bit. It goes right in at the soft part under the fish's gills. But then I have to pull, and the skin and flesh is tougher than I thought.

"I don't want to break it," I say, pulling the nail file out. We have so few tools.

I go back to the creek and search for a rock that is the

right shape. I find one that is round and flat, which I can lift easily with just my one useful arm. I slam it against a boulder until a chunk breaks off, leaving a sharp black edge, and then I go back and line it up against the fish's underside, tugging hard and fast, splitting it open. Instead of dwelling on it, I reach in and scoop out everything I can touch. Intestines spill into my hands, and I drop fistfuls of the fish's guts into the grass beside us.

When I look up again, Celia is holding steady, but she's averted her gaze.

"It's just like sushi," I say, and I'm rewarded by her laugh.

"The last time I had sushi," Celia says, "was in April. Paris was in London for a weekend promoting her new album. We spent the entire weekend holed up in her suite, ordering room service."

We put the fish back into the net and test its weight. It's lighter now, but when I reach down to pick it up with both hands, pain shoots up my hurt arm and I cry out.

I drop to my knees, dizzy from the pain.

When I look at my arm, I can see bright red lines creeping out from under the makeshift bandage I wrapped around the cut yesterday. It's definitely infected. And I've ignored it for too long already.

I feel hands on my back and look up to find Celia.

"What's going on?" she asks. Her voice is too tender, and I'm in too much pain.

A few tears spill down my cheeks.

"My shoulder. I hurt it during the wreck. I think it's worse than I realized."

Celia helps me stand and walks me back toward our little camp. "Okay, well, we won't know until we take a look, right?"

She keeps her voice upbeat, and I'm grateful.

Celia unwraps my arm. When the last layer pulls away, it pulls crusted blood and skin with it, and I flinch at the awful tugging sensation.

Celia sucks in a breath.

"What is it?" I crane my neck to the side for a proper look.

I regret the choice instantly.

My arm is bulging where the cut was, the tissue white and dead. In the gap between skin, where before I could see muscle exposed, there are bright white pearls.

"What the hell is that?" I ask.

"I don't know," Celia says.

"Oh my god, Celia, it's moving." The pearls inside the wound start to wriggle.

"Maggots, I think," Celia tells me. "And your skin is necrotic."

"I don't know what that means," I tell her, staring at the ground.

I can't look at my arm again.

"The tissue is dead, Liv. It needs to be debrided. Removed. Just hold still; I'm going to grab a few things, okay?"

I wait in the grass, defeated and delirious from the pain.

Celia returns with the first aid kit and a can of soda I'd tossed into the bottom of the backpack.

"Here, drink this," she says, popping it open with a hiss.

"Why?" I ask.

"Just do it." She is lining up gauze and the one precious tube of antibiotic ointment we have.

I do what Celia says. The soda is warm, and not exactly refreshing, but it's sweet and fizzy and makes me feel slightly better.

"Hand it over," she says, holding her hand out for the empty can.

She takes the can back to the creek, rinsing it out. She uses the nail file to poke a few holes in the side and then she pulls the can until it breaks apart. The edges are sharp and curved and I realize what she's going to use it for.

"Okay, so this is absolutely going to suck like nothing else in your life," Celia says when she returns and kneels by my arm. "And there's not a damn thing I can do about that except be quick."

"God, Celia. Okay. Just do it."

Before she starts, I think that nothing could be worse than the pain of the infection, the grotesqueness of the injury and the little maggots currently residing inside my skin.

I'm wrong.

When Celia starts scraping the wound out, I scream

through clenched teeth. White-hot burning pain climbs from my arm, ricocheting throughout my body.

"Stop. Stop!" I beg her after just a few seconds of it.

Celia sits back and I get sick. Warm soda splashes all over my sneakers.

"Okay," I say when I'm done. "Keep going."

I don't make another noise as she continues. On the ground beside me is a growing pile of skin and blood and squirming maggots.

I feel a strange tugging on my arm and look up. Celia's cleaned out the wound. It's a bloody mess, but the maggots and the dead flesh are gone.

Underneath them is a pulsing blue mushroom.

"What the hell," I whisper as I realize what the tugging sensation was. "Is it . . . growing out of me?"

Celia gives one last hard pull, wrenching the fungus from my body.

"Yes. It was."

When she's done, Celia steps away for a moment. I'm pretty sure she gets sick, too, but I can't hear it over the pounding in my own head.

"I don't know how to stitch it," she says. "I'm sorry."

"Don't be. We can't sterilize a needle without a fire anyway," I tell her, head balanced on my good arm, which is draped across my bent knees.

She puts ointment on the gauze and wraps my arm, tighter

than I did the first time, and this time with an actual clean cloth. I hope that's enough to stop the infection, because there's no way in hell I'm letting her clean out the wound again. I would absolutely rather die.

She lets me rest for a while, not hurrying me in any way. She's probably worried I'll pass out. I'm a little worried I will, too. But eventually, the pounding in my head abates. When I move my arm, it's tender and raw, but nothing like the throbbing pain it was before.

We follow a different path back downhill after we cross the meadow. It doesn't really matter—there are no trails, just us forging through the softest ground we can find for the sake of Celia's feet. We don't talk much, so the trek is already quiet when I hear it.

Or rather, when I realize what I don't hear.

I stop walking, pulling my end of the net to stop Celia short. When she turns back, confused, I put my finger to my lips.

The forest has gone silent around us.

We stand still for a long time, the fish swinging between us until the muscles in my forearm begin to burn and I have to set it down. Celia silently mirrors my movement.

The bit of the forest to the left of us grows even thicker than the rest of it, and there is a soft blue glow in the darkness. When I point it out to Celia, she shrugs. I slip my sneakers off, and together, barefoot, we move toward the grove.

When we go around the trees thick with vines and ivy, the ground slopes downward, and at the bottom of the trench there is a pond so blue it practically shines, reflecting light onto the trees and creating the glow we saw.

It's beautiful and clear—there is nothing in it besides a few boulders in the bottom. I don't even ask Celia before I climb down the embankment, not stopping until I am inches away. I hold my hand out over the water, and I can feel the cold radiating off it. I dip my finger in, and my skin burns, the water is so cold. I pull it back out with a soft gasp of pain.

Colder than the ocean. Colder than the creek.

It's summer, and yet this small, still pond of water is near freezing.

I feel a different kind of sharp pain on my upper arm, and turn as Celia removes her hand, leaving four small crescents cut into my skin where her nails had just been.

The blue of the pool of water is glimmering across her skin, a soft cerulean reflection in her dark eyes, and it's only when I look past that blue glow that I see her fear. There are tears welling in her eyes, and she lifts her other hand to point.

The boulders in the pond have moved.

They aren't boulders at all. The shadows shift, and the tendrils in the water that my brain had automatically categorized as some sort of aquatic plant turn out not to be that at all. They are attached to the shadow, moving with it.

It is hair.

I watch as an arm stretches out. It ends with a hand not entirely unlike mine, which still hovers just over the water, mirroring the movement of the creature below the surface. But unlike my hand, the one underwater ends in long, curving black claws.

Claws that could tear a man's spine from his body.

It isn't human, and it isn't inhuman, either. It is shaped vaguely like a woman, or the impression of one.

I pull my hand back slowly from where it still hovers above the water's surface.

The tip of my finger is bright red where I touched the water. It looks like I held it to a hot frying pan, and it throbs like a burn, too.

Celia and I don't have to speak the words aloud to understand each other—I rotate my eyes up the hill we just climbed down, and Celia presses her finger across her lips.

Up. Away. Quietly.

We climb out of the grove, and when we are back into the forest and the sunlight, and away from the blue glow of the strange pool of water below, we still don't talk. I lift my sneakers in one hand, and my end of the fishing net in the other. Celia picks up her end and we walk, taking our time. Keeping our feet on moss instead of leaves, on grass instead of branches.

It's quiet between us until long after the forest comes

alive again. A rabbit darts by in the underbrush, startling us. Songbirds flutter in the branches above. The sounds of life are reassuring. Nothing like the silence of the grove we left behind us.

When we finally emerge on the beach, we aren't near our camp. I think we've traveled at least a mile off course, but to be honest, I wasn't paying attention to our direction, only our silence, and our speed.

"I have to tell you something," I say to Celia.

The words surprise me more than her—I hadn't consciously decided that the others needed to know about Vincent, but it was true.

There is something terrible in the woods.

I might have suspected before, but some rational part of me rejected all of that, assured me in the night that it was a mistake, just the worst of my imagination putting puzzle pieces together in a way that wasn't quite right. I just needed to rearrange them, and it would all make sense. I'd convinced myself that Effie and I had missed some vital clue. That there was, as ever before, no such thing as monsters. But I was wrong. There is a monster.

And we are all intruders in its home.

When I finish telling Celia the truth about the condition we found Vincent's remains in, she is pissed.

"That is not okay, Liv. Not out here."

"No, you're right. We didn't—Celia, it didn't seem real." We are making our way back to camp. "It was just so messed up. We didn't know what we were dealing with."

"We still don't," Celia says. "But there was something . . . *terrible* . . . in there. And we can't afford to be hiding things. No more secrets."

Terrible. It is the same word I thought a few moments ago. I don't know what it was about the pond in the forest, only that it made me feel cold, and lonely, and like I'd already plunged into that crystal-clear water, even though all I'd done was touch the tip of one finger to it, creating the tiniest ripple on its smooth surface. But even that small movement was enough to stir the thing below. The terrible, nameless thing.

When we return to camp, Rosa is sitting out on the rocks, with her legs submerged in the ocean.

"She says it's soothing," Miri says. She's tending our little fire. It isn't large enough to work as a signal; we've been too scared to build it large after what happened to Vincent.

Celia and I set down the fish. My whole abdomen is cramping from hurrying down the beach, swinging the weight of it between us. Every muscle in my body is tense and aching when we finally drop the fish next to the fire. At least the pain from my arm isn't as bad. Or rather, it blends right in with all the other pain now.

"Ew, what is that smell?" Miri asks, crinkling her nose. "Oh, gross. Fish?"

"Miri, I swear to Christ—" Celia starts.

"None for you, then," I tell her. I stomp over to the pile of dry branches we've been collecting as we find them and start to build up our fire bigger so we can cook the fish.

"Oh my god, real food," Paris says, walking over to help. "Thank you!"

If she's grossed out by the idea of cooking and eating something we just caught, it doesn't show. Meanwhile, Miri is sitting crisscross on the sand, pouting.

We manage to get the fish turning on a spit over the fire—it is clumsily put together. Effie has her hands on one side, and Paris has hers on the other, just to keep it from collapsing into the fire. But it's working.

I grab the nail clippers from my bag. I can't spend another minute in jeans with wet, sandy bottoms dragging around this entire island, and I use them to cut the material midway up my thigh. I pull the extra material off, tossing it away until I can find a use for it later.

I collapse on the sand, sick and exhausted. Someone plops down next to me, and I open one eye to make sure it isn't Miri.

"How is your foot?" I ask Rosa.

She stretches out her leg to show me. Her foot is covered in iridescent green scales on top, something more like a lizard than a fish, now that I look at it closer. The skin on the bottom of her foot is smooth and tinted gray-green. Her toe doesn't look like it was ever hurt at all.

It just also doesn't look human.

"It doesn't hurt." Rosa shrugs. "It's just so weird."

She's right. It's really strange. When she flexes the arch of her foot and spreads her toes, I see the film of webbing between each of them.

Celia takes Miri to search for more of the figs we ate earlier. They use my sweatshirt to collect them, swinging it like a gathering basket between them on their way back up the beach.

By the time we've all returned to the fire, the fish is practically melting off its bones. Effie's found wide, flat stones, one for each of us to use as plates.

We organize ourselves for the first real meal we've had in days.

The salmon breaks apart on my tongue, steaming hot and tasting vaguely like butter.

"That was the greatest thing I've ever eaten in my life," Miri says.

Five sets of eyes turn to glare at her at once, and Miri only smiles, unashamed.

"I think you've reached peak obnoxious for the day now. Congratulations," I tell her.

"She's right, Mir. Give it a rest, already," Effie whines. "Just say thank you."

"Thank you," Miri says, her succinct, clipped tone somehow still annoying me.

It isn't until the fish is picked to its bones and every last morsel has been sucked off our fingers that Celia catches my gaze, and I nod.

"All right, so listen," she says. "We saw something out there today."

The others give Celia their full attention, and she leans forward, her countenance dead serious for the task at hand.

"There is a monster in the woods," she says.

"Oh, piss off." Miri laughs. "What are you on about now?"

She thinks it's a joke, until Celia starts describing the stillness of the forest. The pool of water in the grove. The creature at the bottom, and how it stirred and reached out a very humanlike hand.

"I'm sure there's an explanation," Rosa says. "It was an animal of some sort. An eel, maybe. We have no idea what lives on this island."

"Exactly," I say. "We don't. But there's more. Effie and I didn't tell you everything before. We did find Vincent, but there wasn't just blood. . . . There were . . . other parts, too."

"Liv, don't—"

"Effie, they have to know. Do you want to explain, or should I?"

Effie rises from the fire and walks down to the ocean, pacing at the water's edge.

I tell them about the tree, the spine, the ribs. Vincent's cigar cutter on the ground. Celia has already described the creature's long claws on the hand in the water, so we just wait while Rosa, Miri, and Paris draw the same conclusions we had.

"We need to get off this island," Miri says. "We shouldn't be making camps and learning how to fish. We should be, I don't know, finding a way to build a boat!"

"We aren't going to sail away from here," I tell her. "We need someone to get us."

She shakes me off and rises from our campfire. "I need to think."

"We shouldn't wander off alone," I start. "Did you listen to anything—"

Miri raises her hand, cutting me off. "I get it, Liv. Murderous creature in the woods. I'll be careful."

She practically runs away from us, like we are the thing she's scared of. When she turns into the woods, I swear under my breath and leap to my feet to chase after her. It's the middle of the day, and we are nowhere near the creature's grove, but we don't know if it stayed in there, or how fast it moves.

I can hear her ahead of me in the woods. She's barefoot, but she's rushing, scared and uncareful of how much noise she's making.

"Miri!" I call out. "Wait for me!"

There's no answer, and I pause, trying to ease another cramp in my abdomen and the ache in my shoulder. I can't keep up with her. When I catch my breath, I realize I can no longer hear the crashing of her footsteps.

"Miri!" I try again. "Miri, where are you?"

I trudge forward in the woods, overheated, exhausted, and unspeakably angry at Miri for putting herself in danger, and for dragging me along, too. I've been walking around feeling guilty for lying, and it turns out that she is the most infuriating—

My line of thinking is cut off abruptly when I step into a clearing and find her. Just like that.

She's standing still, with her back to me.

"Miri, Christ. Don't do that. What is *wrong* with you?

We tell you there's a ravenous monster in the woods and you decide the best idea is to *run into the goddamn woods?*"

Miri doesn't turn. Doesn't move. Doesn't acknowledge me at all, and then I see why.

Across the clearing there is a wolf.

I always thought of wolves as slightly larger than dogs, but the animal in front of us is much larger than that. He is nearly as tall as me, and his muscles ripple under his thick, black-brown fur.

"What do we do?" Miri asks, her voice soft and low.

"Don't. Move," I say. Even as the words leave my lips, the wolf shifts forward, bares his teeth.

Instead of stepping back, I take a step forward. I can feel the moment Miri reaches for me, her fingertips grazing my arm, but she's too far away. I creep between her and the wolf, one careful step at a time.

I don't know why I do it.

I'm furious with her for running off, endangering us both.

But I also should have told her the truth about Vincent. We could have eased everyone into the conversation, instead of ambushing them with confirmation that something awful is on this island with us. Something that is eager to hunt humans and butcher them and display their spines like bloody trophies on trees.

I should have been honest with her, like I promised.

The wolf lowers his huge head, and his shoulders tense.

He will leap at any moment, and tear out my throat, and I'll die here, bleeding out on the pretty blue mushrooms under my sneakers.

There is a scream caught inside of me, buried deep in my chest.

It isn't new. It's older than the wolf standing a few yards away. It's older than our shipwreck, too, though that's kindled its fire these last few days. It's been trapped inside of me for years, building with every little hurt I endured.

It happened once before. I let all my anger fester and grow, until it was this teeming, writhing, living thing. A parasite inside of me, taking everything good. It took only one little unkindness to unleash it. A foster brother, old enough to know better, talking about my pretty sister and the things he wanted to do to her. I'd never felt rage like that before. I don't even remember doing it. I broke his nose and scratched claw marks across his neck and down his chest like a monstrous little demon until they pulled me off him and pinned me down. When I realized what I'd done, when I saw that I'd made a sixteen-year-old boy bleed and cry, the first thing I thought was I hoped it left scars. Something for him to remember me by. *Volatile, violent Violet.*

And now here in this place, all that anger has built back again.

I throw my arms into the air, making myself as big as I can. Then I open my mouth wide and scream every feral ounce of fear I've had trapped inside. I scream away the agony of the shipwreck. I scream off the careful mask I've worn for years of being told it's my fault, I'm the problem, I'll never be good enough. Every bit of loneliness I've carried, which is like a bottomless well of anger.

Because I am a survivor. I made it through the shipwreck. The monster's attack. Having my arm scraped down to the bone. I want to live, and no man or beast is going to take that from me now.

The wolf's ears flatten to his head, and those shoulders ripple, preparing to move. But instead of charging, he takes a step back.

The wolf retreats into the trees, backing away from me and my sudden ferocity.

When he's gone, I drop my arms, breathing heavy, not caring about the noise. If the monster wants me, it knows exactly where I am after that.

Arms wrap around me from behind, and I grasp them at my waist, my nails digging into the tender flesh of Miri's forearms. In a way, she anchors me, her tight grip reminding me of the thing I've been telling myself over and over like a record skipping in my brain.

We're still here.

We're not dead.

We're not dead yet, some terrible part of me whispers back. When I try to peel her arms from around my waist, Miri only tightens her hold on me. Instead, I turn in her arms, and wrap mine around her, too.

"I'm sorry," I say.

"What? Why are *you* sorry?" Her voice is muffled against my neck, and I feel her hot tears run down my chest. "I was awful."

"We should have told you everything about Vincent. So that it wasn't such a shock."

"You're right. This is all your fault. You swore not to lie to me."

"That's why I'm sorry," I repeat.

Miri steps back and covers her face with both hands. It reminds me so much of the way she covers her mouth when she laughs that I can't help but smile at it.

"Stop it," she says through her fingers. "Stop apologizing. I can't believe you just did that."

Miri is fully sobbing now.

"It's okay, we're okay. We didn't get hurt."

"Shut *up*, Liv. Just stop talking. You are right, and you're never scared, and it's so goddamned bloody annoying that you've saved all of our lives on this godforsaken island, like we are these—" Miri hiccups, interrupting herself. "Like we are these *useless* . . ."

I'm struggling to hear what Miri is even saying, she's crying so hard.

"Useless rich girls," she finally finishes. "But I'm very cross with you for lying and very confused and I want to slap you for putting yourself in that much danger and I also think I want to kiss you."

Miri continues to cry, softer now. She drops her hands and leans forward, pressing her face into my uninjured shoulder and letting her tears run freely down the front of me. They slip down my shirt across my chest, but I don't make her move.

My heart has only just stopped racing from the adrenaline after encountering the wolf, but it starts to beat faster again now.

Because of her.

"Well, which is it?" I ask.

"What?" She looks up, sniffling and pulling up her shirt to wipe her face. Her hair is loose, and wavy tendrils of it cling to the sweaty sides of her face and neck. A feverish pink flush has crept from her cheeks all the way down to her chest. She's a complete mess, and she's still so pretty that my chest hurts when I look at her.

"Which do you want to do? The former or the latter?"

"Both," she snaps. "Neither." She's quiet for a moment longer. "The latter, Liv."

"Wait, is 'latter' second?" I ask.

Miri closes the distance between us.

When she kisses me, I can taste her tears.

16

Miri's lips are chapped, but the moment she pulls away, I miss the touch of them on me.

She laughs even though she's still sort of crying, too, and then covers her mouth to hide it.

"I love that," I tell her. I can't keep it to myself any longer.

"What?" she asks.

"When you laugh, you cover your mouth. It's, like, stupid cute."

"Don't call me cute," she says, frowning. "It's an old habit. I used to have a massive gap between my front teeth. The boys at primary school called me Peter."

"Peter?"

"Rabbit."

I start to smile, and Miri gives me a look deadlier than the one I got from the wolf.

"Don't you dare laugh at that."

I bite my lips. "I wouldn't."

"And don't call me cute. I'm a serious, respected artist. I am a woman with serious wants and needs and a serious life. I'm not *cute*."

"Never again," I promise.

Miri must forgive me because her lips find mine again for another kiss.

"This doesn't change things," she says when she pulls away.

"Obviously," I tell her. "You're still a complete brat."

"And you're a liar, Everly Whitlock."

My sister's name on her lips is a sharp pain in my chest. She's right. I am a liar.

Miri's hand finds its way into mine.

I should tell her the whole truth now.

"We should probably get back," I say. "Before the others worry. Or that wolf comes back with reinforcements."

"Good point," Miri agrees.

We make our way back down through the forest, finally breaking through the thick foliage onto the beach. As we walk down the shore, I feel a warm tickle on my leg and look down. There is a rivulet of blood running down the inside of my knee.

"What the hell," I mutter, and then I realize exactly what it is.

My period's started.

I guess I wasn't cramping from running earlier. I just didn't even think of it out here, a little distracted by trying to not die. There's nothing I can do about it. The blood reaches the top of my sneaker, leaving a bright red drop of crimson on the muddy white fabric.

I drop Miri's hand and head down to the ocean to splash water on my legs.

"Perfect. Just perfect," I mutter angrily, practically stomping my feet as I go.

"Liv, are you hurt? You're bleeding."

"I got my period," I call back.

"Oh. Wow. That is truly awful timing," she says.

"Right, well, I'm starting to think Mother Nature can be a little vindictive." I throw my hands up on the last word, indicting the entire island for the crime in my abdomen.

"Is that the real reason you unleashed holy hell on that wolf back there? PMS?" Miri asks. She joins me in the waves, and I shove at her playfully.

"Honestly, maybe it was," I say, laughing.

We are nearly nose to nose, practically the same height. I am so caught up in the hazy gray-green of her eyes that I don't realize we have an audience.

"What's all this?" a voice asks behind us.

We startle apart from each other and find Celia watching us from a few yards away, one hand on her popped hip and a knowing smile on her lips.

Miri and I talk over each other, rushing to explain, but Celia just laughs.

"You don't have to explain yourselves to *me*, right?" she says. "You must know I get it."

"There's nothing to get," I say, but it's a lie.

I know it, Miri knows it, and Celia absolutely knows it, too.

When we get back to camp, we start preparing for another night. I shred part of the discarded pieces of denim from my jeans for a makeshift pad, and Effie graciously gives me her pajama pants to wear.

We ate the entire fish earlier, leaving us with figs and the last of the protein bars for dinner. But when I call everyone for food, only Effie, Rosa, and Miri join me.

"Where are Celia and Paris?" I ask, but no one has seen them since Miri and I got back.

The sun is starting to set.

We split up to walk the shore. Miri and Effie head south while Rosa and I head north along the sand, keeping as wide a berth as possible between us and the trees now that the forest is getting dark. I'm not sure it even matters. We don't know that the creature only comes out at night.

"What's that?" I point ahead of us, where something large has washed ashore.

I jog up the beach, stopping when I reach a large wooden crate. It has a document stapled to it, and it's laminated, but water has gotten inside the plastic, and all the ink runs like mascara-soaked tears down the page. It probably listed the contents.

The crate is nailed shut.

Rosa grabs a long, thick branch from the edge of the forest and wedges it into the open hole handle on the side, pushing it until it's pressed firmly against the lid.

"On three," she says, and I place one hand beside the two of hers on the branch. My other arm is still mostly useless.

"One, two, three."

We press at the same time, and the crate creaks, protesting the pressure. But the lid budges, the nails lifting a centimeter out of the wood. It's all waterlogged, and softened, otherwise I don't think we could do this with our strength alone.

"Again," I tell Rosa.

On our third push, it gives, cracking open as the wood releases the nails. Rosa climbs up and pries it off, looking down into the crate.

"Is it food?" I call up, so hopeful I can almost taste it on my tongue.

"If he wasn't already dead, I'd kill him," Rosa says.

She reaches down into the crate and pulls out a cloth bag. She unties the silk ribbon knot at the top of it and dumps the contents right onto the beach.

A dress falls out.

I lift it out of the sand. "What the hell?" I ask.

"They're the costumes, Liv. Dresses, slips, goddamn *ballet* shoes." As Rosa rants, she pulls more soaked canvas bags from the crate, dropping them into the sand.

"But why?" I ask, sorting through the items.

"Tax-write-off shit," Rosa says. "The same reason he wanted *us* on the ship instead of the plane: so his fancy yacht could be wrapped up in his production company."

"He was the worst," I say, looking at the pile in the sand, wishing it was food, or the emergency phone.

"Here," Rosa says, handing me a few bags, taking the rest herself. "Let's come back for the rest later."

"It's not food, but it's not completely useless," I tell her as we make our way back to camp. "We can layer the clothes for warmth. The bags can carry fruit. The ribbons might help secure our makeshift fishing net."

"Fair enough. Though, for the record, I still hate his guts."

"No argument there." But in my head, I can't help but recall the image of his actual guts, dripping down the side of a tree trunk.

When we get back, only Effie and Miri are there.

"They aren't back yet?" Rosa asks, dismayed.

"No, they're not." Effie is pacing near the shelter. "And we thought you were gone, too. Could everyone kindly stop disappearing on this murderous island for a minute?"

Effie twists her hair up into a knot on top of her head, only to pull it back down a minute later. She paces the beach, leaving an infinity sign in the sand with her footprints. She tugs and twists knots into her hair as she goes.

"Hey, Effie, I'm sure they're all right," Miri says.

"Well, good, Mir. As long as you're sure."

Effie stops walking. She tilts her head back and lets all that bright red hair go falling down her back again. "I'm sorry," she says with her eyes closed. "I'm worried."

"I know," Miri says. "But they aren't yours to worry about, Ef. Come sit down. Eat."

While we start our meal, Rosa and I describe the massive crate we found up the shore, and the ridiculous contents inside. I have plans to take the ribbons out of the bags and make more nets for fish.

"We can move rocks in the creek, to sort of trap the bigger fish," Rosa says. "Though we might want to try for a few smaller ones instead, so it's easier to carry them."

There is a crashing sound just behind our shelter, branches and brush being crushed under something moving fast.

We've barely gotten to our feet when Paris and Celia erupt from the woods. They collapse onto the sand, laughing, trying to catch their breath.

"What the *hell* are you two thinking? It's already dark," Effie says.

"Relax, Mum," Celia says. She doesn't look ashamed in the smallest bit. In fact, she's practically glowing. Paris is no better, giggling and burying her face against Celia's arm.

That's when I notice that their clothes are wrong. Celia

is trying to rebutton her pajama shirt as inconspicuously as possible.

She's very bad at it, missing the same button three times.

"Oh, stop." Paris smacks her hand away and fixes Celia's buttons. Celia untangles a twig from her hair in return.

"Oh my god!" Miri stands to her full height, and I think she's trying to look stern. "Is that really a priority?"

"How could it not be?" Celia says from the sand. "We're probably all going to die anyway."

"Next time you want privacy, just use the shelter," I say. "The rest of us will go for a walk or something. I hardly think an orgasm is worth dying over."

"Spoken like someone who hasn't had one," Paris says. Her tone is playful, teasing even, but I flush bright red in an instant.

"Besides," Celia says. "I think we've got our priorities dead straight. Right, Paris?"

"Let's review." Paris holds up her fingers as she ticks off all the forces of heaven and earth that seem to be conspiring against us. "One. We are clearly stuck here on this island. We can't call for help because the only *briefly* surviving adult among us couldn't keep track of the emergency phone. Two. We have no food, except what we can hunt and gather ourselves, and our collective experience in that area is—what would you say, Celia? Zip? Nada?"

"Zilch," Celia says.

"Three. We've just learned there is a literal monster hunting us and displaying our bones like trophies."

"So we just thought, what the hell? We ought to lean into whatever joys we can find out here," Celia says. "It's not going to be food, or a warm bed, or a hot shower. But it could be love, or sex, or, I don't know, art!"

"Art?" Effie says, perking up a bit. "What do you mean?"

"We still have the Bard," Celia says. She crosses to the shelter and lifts the mostly dry book from where it's been lying out in the sun all day. "We have two of the most talented actresses on earth. You said it last night, Ef. We need to read. And create. And love on each other while we can."

"They're right," Rosa says. She stands right at the water's edge, letting the waves lap at her strange, scaled foot. Her fever broke, and now she's running hot; a light sheen of sweat covers her even though she's stripped down to just her sports bra and a pair of Celia's shorts that washed up. "We might be here for a while. Maybe for the rest of our lives, however long that is. What's the point if all we do is barely survive? 'Cause I'm gonna be honest, that's what I've been doing for years out there." Rosa points behind her, at the sea. "And it wasn't working for me off the island, either."

We are all quiet with that for a minute. By *out there,* Rosa means the entire rest of the world. But she's right. I think that's all I've been doing for years, too. Just surviving.

It was aching. Lonely. It hurts to never belong to anyone.

"Can I have that, Celia?" I ask, reaching for the book.

I find the part I want and pass it to Miri.

"Do you mind?"

Miri reads for a bit, and a smile perches on her lips, as light and fleeting as a hummingbird. "Not at all."

While we gather around our fire, Miri reads over what I've asked of her, nibbling on a protein bar. Celia helps me pull the wooden plank roof off our shelter, temporarily, and lay it out on the sand.

"All the world's a stage," she says, examining our handiwork. "Or something vaguely resembling a stage, if you squint your eyes and use your imagination, I suppose."

Miri finishes reading and shuts the book. I wonder if she really memorized it that quickly. I watch as Miri steals a hair tie from Paris and twists her hair on each side, securing the pieces in place at the back of her head.

When she steps onto the wooden board—her stage—she changes.

It should be impossible to forget who she is or where we are, but right before my eyes, it's like a kind of mask slides into place on Miri's face, and then nothing can penetrate it.

She truly looks transformed.

Her first lines are nearly a whisper, and we all lean in to catch her words like fireflies in the night. If we don't hurry, they'll be gone. A fleeting kind of magic.

"Our revels now are ended. These our actors, as I foretold

you, were all spirits . . ."

As Miri speaks, it doesn't take very long for me to be drawn into her world. There is no set. No costume. No fellow actors. And yet she commands our attention fully.

I'd seen her in movies, but there is nothing like watching her perform right in front of me. I'd seen a glimpse of it on the *Bianca,* and again now. Miri makes it seem effortless, authentic.

"The cloud-capped towers, the gorgeous palaces, the solemn temples, the great globe itself . . ."

Her voice carries across the beach, echoing against the trees. Miri isn't scared of what might hear her. I don't think she's even here at all.

The sunset burns behind her, with long fissures of maroon and vermilion cracking open a lavender sky. It's the curtain lining her stage. Miri stands like a muse incarnate against the backdrop. She's Persephone in a clandestine meeting with Hades. She's Helen, unwittingly about to inspire a war in her name.

"She's extraordinary," I whisper aloud. I don't care if the others hear me. For the first time since our ship tore itself apart on the rocks of this strange island with its terrible monster, I'm not thinking about being hungry or cold or lost or in pain.

I am still feeling all those things, but Miri offers a respite, and for a moment that loneliness I've known my whole life is gone. Here, in this place, I am whole, and adequate. I am enough, just as I am. When I remember how it felt to kiss Miri earlier, to stop her crying and feel the eager press of her lips against mine, I feel a surge of joy, slow and sweet in my veins.

"We are such stuff as dreams are made on, and our little life is rounded with a sleep."

I see the moment she comes back to us. Drawn back into her mortal form from the ethereal creature she'd been while performing.

Miri's eyes find mine, and I know with deep-rooted clarity that the others are right.

There is more to this than mere survival.

When I wake in the night, the fire has nearly burned itself out. Only a few embers remain, glowing blood orange in the sandpit.

The wind is howling outside our small enclosure, but it isn't raining. Temperatures dropped quickly once the sun set, and we pulled the dresses out of the crate for warmth, piling them onto us like blankets. Except for me and Rosa.

Ever since our fevers broke, we've been running hot, even when the wind picked up and Celia's arms were covered in goose bumps from the chill. I've slept in only a slip—a thin gossamer silk undergarment meant for the production. Even that clings to me, sticking to the slippery sheen of sweat covering my body.

It's too hot inside our shelter, cloying and claustrophobic from so many bodies in so small a space. I need air. I climb over the others as carefully as I can, extracting myself slowly from the tangle of arms and legs.

Outside, I walk to the water's edge, only stopping when the ocean reaches my bare toes. The moon is high above me, and thick gray clouds are on the dark horizon. I watch a lightning storm play out in the distance.

I roll my stiff shoulder, testing it. I'm terrified to look under the bandages. My arm doesn't itch like before, and the pain has stayed a kind of dull ache, replacing the throbbing pain from earlier that made my stomach roll with nausea every time I moved it.

The wind on the water makes the same keening wails it made the night we wrecked. It could almost be mistaken for music. Funeral dirges carrying the tales of sunken ships and drowned sailors.

When I finally turn back toward our shelter, I see it.

It is standing in the woods, just beyond the reach of the moonlight, which projects strange shadows on the branches and leaves around it. It gives the impression of movement, though the creature stays still, less than a dozen yards from where everyone sleeps.

It stands upright, vinelike hair streaming down its sides. I wasn't wrong before—it is not human, but it is humanlike. It looks like it crawled from the pages of a fairy tale. As old as language itself. More ancient than trees. Something eldritch and haunting, and yet known. As familiar as the sand beneath my toes.

There are words for creatures like this. *Druid*. *Witch*.

Siren. All relegated categorically to the realm of folklore and mythology. It is nearly impossible to merge the idea of this creature's existence with *here* and *now* and *real*.

I can't tell if her eyes are open, or even if she has eyes, but I know she's aware of me. My calf muscles burn from holding so still for so long. Watching and waiting.

When I shift my weight in the sand, she moves. Her head tilts to one side, almost as though she's trying to listen for something. Then she turns away, back toward the darkest parts of the forest behind her.

I don't know what compels me. It's like my feet move of their own accord, following some invisible path trailing behind the creature. I know where to go even when I lose sight of her in the thick trees.

What must be miles later, deep in the woods, there is a familiar blue glow.

The creature's grove.

When I follow her inside, she is waiting for me at the edge of the water. It's only when I start to descend the slope down to her that she steps into the pool, slipping so quickly beneath the surface it's like she's made of fluid herself.

I follow, beads of sweat pouring down my neck and pooling between my breasts. The moment my toes touch the water, it ripples, shimmering beneath me.

When it stills, the surface is as reflective as a mirror. I see myself, wild-eyed in an ivory slip, barefoot, with streaks of dirt across my face where I brushed against tree branches in the dark. My dark hair is in a rough braid that hangs over my shoulder—anything to keep it off me during the strange, fever-pitch heat that's consumed my body for hours.

The Liv in the reflection moves, though I do not. She reaches for the bandage on her arm, slowly unraveling the gauze, letting it fall away. Beneath it, the wound is healed, except for a white line crossing the skin, brighter than a normal scar. She puts her nails against the line and pulls until a silver thread comes out, unraveling me like she's unfastening my skin.

Then she tugs the string, once, hard, and the wound on my arm splits open. Searing pain lances through my shoulder, and a crimson stain spreads across the gauze. I reach for the end of the fabric and pull it off, letting it fall to the pool below.

When I look back to the water, the mirrored surface is gone, and it's only me standing there, holding the gaping wound on my arm closed with my fingers. I sink to my knees in the pool of freezing water. I expect it to burn my skin, like it did my fingertips. Instead, the coolness of the water is soothing my overheated body as pain radiates through it from my arm.

Small mushrooms are bursting out of my skin where it opened. They are as blue as the edge of a hot flame. When I reach to pull them out, a hand closes over my own, stopping me. Thin fingers wrap around my fingers.

Not claws after all, but long black nails.

I lift my head slowly. I can feel her breath on my face, and I know she's right in front of me. But the moment my eyes rise to meet hers, there is a flash of blue light, blindingly bright all around me.

I'm back on the beach again, standing in the waves.

My feet are numb from the cold, and the fire continues to glow embers near the others, all sound asleep. I'm so tired I can barely make the trek back up the sand, half dragging my feet that have lost most of their feeling. My eyes go to the place in the forest where I saw the creature earlier, but there is only darkness. I wonder if I dreamed it. If I imagined it, like when my fever peaked and I saw my own memories in the DeLucas' kitchen, growing wild in the forest.

My fingers go to my arm, and the bandages are gone. I can feel the foreign shapes of mushrooms emerging from my skin, up and down my arm. I hold my arm above me in the moonlight. There are more of them now.

In all the places where I had scars on my arm, there are now small half-moon crescents of mushrooms. Each burn mark has been replaced by sprouting lichen, curving around the shape of my arm like shelves stacked on top of each other. The same way they grow on the side of a tree.

Part of me wants to scrape it off. I'm not sure why I don't, except for the image of that hand in my mind, wrapping around my own, stopping me. And the fact that the longer I leave it alone, the better my arm starts to feel.

I can't stand the idea of crawling back into the shelter with the others—my feet might be numb, but the rest of me is still unbearably hot. I curl up in the sand, my eyes on the river of green sky and stars above me.

My first instinct is to keep it all to myself. I'm still half convinced I made it up in my head. *Why stop now?* Effie had asked when I told her I didn't want to lie.

But I have a better reason than the promise I made to Miri. I just don't want to do it anymore. I don't want to be that person who must lie and steal to get what everyone else seems to acquire so easily. The girl who never feels deserving, or enough.

That girl is an island. She'll be alone forever.

I don't want to be her anymore, and that means no more secrets.

No more secrets.

It's the mantra I fall asleep to, and it's still echoing in my head in the morning when Miri gently wakes me, her smile above me. It's still half dark, that pink-gray sky that means the sun is rising on the far side of the island. Light is on the way.

"Thought I lost you," she says, helping me sit up.

No more secrets.

I show Miri my arm, and she takes it in her hands,

examining it closely as I explain what happened overnight. And Miri listens. When the others wake, she repeats the story as fact, not weaving her doubts or questioning the legitimacy of what I saw and heard. Suddenly I'm not sure if I was ever truly a liar, or if I'd just never been the kind of girl that people believed.

Celia examines my arm, pressing her fingers just above and below the light blue lichen, watching how my skin pales and then returns color.

"Your circulation looks healthy, but it's really bizarre," she says.

I raise my eyebrows and hold up my arm growing its own mushrooms as if to say, *I think we've established that.*

"No, I mean, besides that. It's these older scars that don't make sense, considering what we've seen with Rosa, too. Scurvy can cause old scars to reopen like this. It breaks down the collagen. But scurvy would take months to have symptoms like that. And I'm pretty sure the fruit you found has enough vitamin C that we'll be fine."

"Celia, I don't understand."

"Your arm and Rosa's foot are both injuries that happened *here*. If it's a parasite or some weird infection or something, then at least it's consistent. Your completely healed scars don't match the pattern."

"So, what do we do?"

"Well, we definitely need more data."

"If Celia can scientific method our way off this island, she will," Paris says.

But I'm lost in thought, considering Celia's last words. *More data*. That means more injuries, I suppose, which are completely unpredictable.

I reach for my backpack, grabbing the first aid tin and digging out the sewing kit. I remove one of the needles and prick the tip of my finger. A single drop of blood wells.

"Was that wise?" Paris asks from her seat beside Celia.

"If a tiny pinprick is enough to kill us here, I'm not sure we're long for this world," Celia tells her. "Tell me if anything happens as soon as you notice it, okay?"

"Right." I pop my finger into my mouth, sucking the droplet of blood off.

"I want to show you something." Celia pulls one of my notebooks from my backpack and opens it. There is a grid on the page, measured in careful, even increments and labeled by letter on one axis, number on the other.

"What is it?"

"We're going to make a map. We need a better sense of where we are, where the creature lives, and what the hell else is on this island. We could be missing something important."

We'd circled the entire island's perimeter the day after the wreck. Celia and Paris went one way, and Effie and Miri went the other while I stayed to watch over Rosa. They'd only managed to confirm that it was, in fact, an island. And that there were no signs of human life anywhere in sight.

"I'll go." Paris kneels beside Celia, her arm sneaking across Celia's lap in a possessive gesture. I think what happened to me last night has everyone on edge.

Rightfully so.

"Me too," I offer. "I think I can direct us around the grove well enough."

"That's a good plan," Effie says. Then she leans in and quiets her voice. "Listen, Rosa wants to dive again."

Rosa is back at the water's edge, her feet submerged. Miri stands beside her, talking softly.

"Why? Does she think there's more to salvage from the wreck? What about her foot?"

"I don't know. She wants to be in the water, and figures she might as well be useful, and try the wreck again."

"Okay. If that's what she wants."

"I'll go out with her," Effie says. "Miri can watch from shore in case there's trouble."

We finish the last of the crackers and eat a few figs each for breakfast. We should try for another fish later, too. I offer Celia my sneakers. We've been taking turns with them since they're the only shoes that made it onto the island. I leave my sweatshirt with Miri for Effie when she gets out of the water. Rosa is still running hot like I am—every beat of my pulse is like a surge of new warmth through my body. It's stifling.

We walk for at least an hour down the shore before anything changes. Then ahead of us, the beach ends, and a rocky climb begins. We move even slower here, taking our time to make sure our footing is secure with every step. There is seaweed covering the lowest rocks where the tide covers them at certain hours, and the rocks are slick and slippery.

When we reach the top, we can look back up the coast. There is a long stretch of sand and rock, and the way the island curves, we can see the entire strip of beach at once.

The island is shaped like a crescent, and our shelter is toward the center of the inlet. I can make out the orange flicker of our small fire, the white flash of the ship's hull out in the water—though even that is nearly disguised by the white foam of cresting waves all around the island. The crescent must extend in a full circle, but the outer rim is mostly underwater. The rocks protect our coast from rougher waves. They're also what we wrecked on.

No one would see our camp from the air. It would just look like more ocean around a nameless, empty island. I remind myself to build up a larger signal fire when I get back. It's not like the creature doesn't know where to find us, and it might be our only chance at being seen.

"Onward?" Paris asks.

When we finally reach the far side of the island, we don't find another curving beach. We find a cliff. It is a sheer, steep drop down to rock and ocean below. The entire island must slope toward where we wrecked.

How lucky it is that we landed on that side, and not this one.

Celia sits on the ground and sketches out the outline of the island, as far as we know it. She marks our camp and the wreck and cliffs. There is another slope on the northern end, a hill that leads up to its highest point. "We need to get up there eventually," Celia murmurs, adding its rough location to her map. I also take a guess at where the creature's grove was, and the creek.

"Let's cut back through the woods to get to camp so we can fill in some of the map," Celia says.

"But what about the . . . the thing?" Paris asks.

"That's on the northern end of the island. We should be all right down here. I'm guessing it's nocturnal based on our interactions with it so far."

When Celia finishes drawing, we turn back, this time trekking through the forest instead of sticking to the coast. Paris sings softly as we go. It's just a children's song. Nothing fancy. But I'm glad she chose it. It's comforting.

When we are about halfway back, Paris suddenly cries out. She was leading our small fellowship, and I look up to see a cloud of blue-gray dust rise from the ground. It envelops her whole head, and she starts to cough so hard she doubles over.

Celia and I pull her away from the dust. She's coughing

harder, dragging breaths, and drops to her knees with a gasp.

"Paris, love, you have to calm down," Celia says. "You are panicking. You have to breathe."

I rub my hand against the small of Paris's back, and I feel the moment her coughing lessens—slowly, so slowly. But eventually her breathing evens. When she faces us, her eyes are closed and tears are streaming down her face. Celia moves to wipe them away and smears red across her cheek. They aren't tears. They're blood.

18

Paris has beads of blood running down her face from her eyes. Her ears and nose are bleeding, too. Celia wipes the rust droplets away the best she can, using her thumbs to swipe under Paris's eyes and nose, her palm to dab at the blood leaking from her ears.

"I can't open my eyes," Paris says, her voice raw and whisper-soft. Fear threads through her words like a sharp whistle. It's like the dust has hollowed out the parts of her that make her substantial and real, leaving only a scared shell behind, echoing all the sounds.

"Can you walk?" Celia asks. "We can lead you, but we need to get back to camp."

"Yeah. Yes. I can walk. Let's get out of here."

"One sec," I say. "Don't move. I'm not going far, okay?"

Paris nods, and I carefully edge back to the thing that hurt her. It's a round puffball fungi of some kind. It is an inky navy color on the outside—but the inside is bright indigo, vibrant and covered in the same blue dust that hit Paris. When she stepped on it, it split open, releasing all its spores into the air.

I hurry back, and we help Paris to her feet.

I expect the journey to go slow with Paris depending on us for guidance, but she gives herself over to us completely. Her trust in Celia is implicit.

We make our way back as fast as we can.

It's only toward the end, when I can already see the break in the trees ahead and hear the sound of the waves on the rocky coast, that Paris sags against me a little heavier.

"Just tired," she says, leaning her head on my shoulder. Her breath on my neck comes in quick pants. "Everything hurts."

"Celia?" I ask.

"Myalgia," Celia says. "Muscle pain. Shortness of breath. It's okay. What about any weakness?"

Paris lifts her arm, but the movement is lethargic.

"S'wrong with me," she mumbles.

"That mushroom was toxic," Celia says. "You inhaled the spores in that dust."

"Dying?" she asks.

Celia looks at me over Paris's lolling head on my shoulder. She doesn't know. She's terrified.

"Absolutely not," she says. "It's just going to make you sleepy and sore. Your chest might hurt a while from all the coughing. And you'll probably get—"

"Hang on." Paris shudders and leans over to throw up on the sand at the same moment we break through the trees onto the beach and leave the forest behind.

"Nauseated," Celia finishes.

The sound of Paris getting sick draws the attention of Effie and Miri, who are tending the fire and organizing items I can't make out from this distance. Effie reaches us first, taking my place. She loops an arm around Paris and helps Celia carry her the rest of the way.

We settle her in at the camp, layering dresses across her for warmth. I press my palm to her face—she's already hot with fever, and it hasn't even been an hour since her exposure. I don't know what it means for her to be so sick so fast. But acute reactions are rarely a good sign. Celia has to bribe her for several long minutes to drink enough water. The more she flushes this out of her system, the better.

I use some of our clean water to rinse her eyes as best I can and wipe up the blood and the few specks of blue dust left on the bridge of her nose.

I tear off a strip of material from one of the clean, dry slips. The silk will protect her eyes, and hopefully encourage her to keep them closed, instead of constantly fighting the urge to open them.

Celia helps me tie the silk at the back of her head.

"I'll stay with her," she says.

"I'll be nearby, so just call out if you need anything."

She doesn't even answer, just sinks farther into the cushions of our shelter. I think they're both asleep before I even rise off my knees.

"What the hell was it?" Effie asks when I join her and Miri on the beach.

Rosa has returned, too. Her eyes are fixed on the woods. Watching, waiting.

"It was some kind of mushroom. She stepped right on it and inhaled, like, a whole cloud of dust and spores."

"This island is set on killing us, isn't it?" Effie snaps.

"Well, not entirely," Miri says. "Rosa's thing was pretty helpful."

"What are you talking about?" I ask.

"Here, look at this." Miri pulls me around the rocks that contain our camp and where Paris sleeps.

On the other side is treasure.

"Oh, wow." I drop to my knees. I reach out slowly, like the image before me might shudder and blow away with the breeze, like a desert mirage.

We have bags. Five of them, including mine, right in front of me. I unzip mine right away, and squeal like a child with excitement at the contents. Everything is in here. It's wet, but it's here, and it will dry. My clothes, my toiletries case. *My toothbrush.*

I feel the hot burn of tears in my eyes and brush them

away. This little glimpse of familiarity is undoing me.

"How?" I look up to find Miri grinning at my reaction.

"Rosa has been in and out all morning. She is faster and can stay under for a while. I swear she's—"

"Stop it," Effie snaps, catching up with us. "Stop, Miri."

Miri shrugs. "Then you explain it."

"She thinks the rash made Rosa better in the water," Effie explains to me. She clenches her jaw so tight I can see the tension in her neck, and I'm guessing Effie and Miri were arguing this most of the time we were gone.

"It's not a 'rash.' It's *scales,* Ef. Literal fish scales. And webbed toes. And there's no other explanation," Miri says.

"How about: She's better rested? She's been eating? She isn't on the verge of death this time?"

Effie makes a good point. But it is also very weird that Rosa sprouts scales and now can't stay away from the water.

"Maybe we can just be grateful to have some real clothes and not be so analytical, just this once," I suggest. The Knight sisters fighting with each other is the last thing we need right now.

"Whatever," Effie says. "Miri can keep her delusions. It hardly matters out here."

Effie goes back to the camp, tending the fire and adding more wood, even though I'd just done that when I left the shelter.

"I think it's changing us," Miri says to me once Effie is

far enough away from us.

"Obviously it's changing us," I tell her. My arm is covered in evidence.

Miri is quiet for a moment. I can feel the energy coming off her in waves. She is dying to say more. She just doesn't want me to yell at her like Effie just did. I stop organizing my drenched belongings and turn to give her my full attention.

She's kneeling closer to me than I realized. Turns out she does have freckles. Not nearly so many as her sister, but a little dusting of them across the bridge of her nose.

"Just say it, Miri," I tell her.

"Maybe it's not *all* terrible."

"You mean the fact that I am turning into a toadstool isn't terrible?"

"You aren't," Miri says. "Look at your arm. It's healing."

I've been ignoring it. The last time I studied the injury closely, it was bursting with maggots. But when I look at it now, it's clear that she's not wrong.

The edges of the cut are still tender, but the skin around it is pink and healthy, not the deathly white it had been when it was infected and dying. The blue mushrooms are still there, but they've stopped growing. The little strands of their roots have spread out, mycelium weaving into my skin like capillaries. I can no longer tell where my skin ends and the fungus begins.

It's part of me.

When we return to the others, Miri slips her hand into mine and squeezes tight. Twice. I think to make sure I know it was intentional.

I'm sure the others notice, but no one teases tonight. We are too worried about Paris for anything like that. We eat our figs and the last of the peanut butter and pass around extra clothes from our bags that have dried in time for nightfall.

Miri, Effie, and Celia pull them on.

Rosa and I are still too warm to wear anything but the loose slips from the costumes crate. The silk is cool and soft and now familiar against my skin. Soothing, even.

Paris fights the layers we try to pull onto her.

When I press my fingers to the inside of her bare wrist, her pulse is sluggish, with long lulls between the rolling rhythm of her blood, as though the toxin has made it thick as honey. She is burning up with a fever, and she can barely tolerate the feel of anything on her skin. We give her and Celia the shelter, and Celia helps her change into only a slip, too.

Finally, she rests. She whimpers occasionally in her sleep.

It takes me hours to sleep, and I know my tossing and turning must be disturbing the others. Eventually, Miri rises from the sand across from me and curls up next to me, her arm stubbornly wrapped around my torso, her stiff posture almost daring me to protest.

I'm finally able to settle.

It feels like only seconds pass before I am jolted awake again.

Before I even open my eyes, I know that everything is different. There is no crackling fire. No golden glow of its light on my eyelids. The ocean is different, too. I can hear the lapping waves, but only barely, dulled by distance.

I open my eyes and find the thick canopy of trees above me.

I'm in the forest.

It is nearly dawn. I see gray-pink clouds above in the patches visible through the canopy. The sun hasn't quite breached the island. I turn to my left and find Paris. My fingers instantly wrap around her wrist, and I'm rewarded with the quick, reassuring beat of a strong pulse beneath them.

My other hand throbs, and I lift it up.

The tip of my finger has erupted in growth overnight. My skin all around the place where I pricked it with the needle has been replaced by soft blue folds. Twists of something fleshy, blue, veined, and layered. I touch it and wince at the tenderness.

It's like the growths on my arm, only this time it's entirely made of my skin and my veins. My own flesh and blood, contorted into something new.

I lower my hand and look around. The others are here, too, lined up on the other side of Paris. Celia, Miri, Rosa, Effie. Everyone is wearing only thin white slips, even those who went to sleep in layers and sweaters. I slowly become aware of the soft blue glow reflecting off the silk.

I turn to find a familiar tangle of branches and briars, lit from within by the shimmer of light on water. We are in the monster's grove.

ACT III

Disco Inferno

Hell is empty, and all the devils are here.
—*The Tempest*, Act I, Scene II

I'm aware of every sound we make.

The faint snore coming from Miri, whose face is hidden beneath her arm. The rustle of leaves under Celia as she stirs. Effie must be dreaming. She's mumbling, softly, almost under her breath, the words unintelligible. Rosa is curled up again—she sleeps like a small child. It makes her seem so much younger than she is.

And then Paris, silent beside me, and still wearing the strip of cloth tied over her eyes, but I know the moment she's awake. I feel her pulse spike with awareness under my fingertips.

"Shh," I whisper, squeezing her wrist between my fingers. "I'm here."

She sits up slowly, and I match her movements. I'm scared to make any noise, but I need to warn the others where we are.

"It's sleeping," Paris says. Her voice is raw, barely more than a whisper.

Hardly any light has penetrated the trees yet. We are in the shadows, and I struggle to make out the expression on her face with her eyes still covered. I only see the dark outline of her profile.

"What?" I ask. "How could you know that?"

"I hear it," she says. "Don't you hear it? It's in the water."

"No, I don't hear it," I say, my frustration edging into my voice.

My hands go to the knot at the back of her head, untying the ribbon of soft silk that was protecting her eyes. When she turns to face me, I startle.

It's her eyes. They are no longer the bright amber brown they were yesterday. They are blue. They are paler than the mushrooms that grow all over the island. Lighter than the shining reflection of the monster's lair. The same crystalline white-blue as ice. I lean away from her, crushing leaves and leaning on Miri, who starts to stir. "Paris," I start to tell her, but Miri sits up behind me.

"Where the hell are we?" Miri asks. She hasn't seen it before, but her gaze fixes on the glowing pool of water, and I know she's put it together for herself.

"Shh," I say. "We have to be quiet. It's in there. Can you wake them?" I gesture toward the others, sleeping beyond my reach.

Miri nods and starts with Effie right beside her.

Paris tucks a strand of curly pink hair behind her ear. Her

ears are different, too. She must feel it because her hand stays there, curving around its new shape—wider, more delicate, so thin I can see light through it, and slightly pointed.

"I can hear . . . *everything*," she whispers, and now, finally, there is fear in her voice matching mine. "What is this? Liv, what is wrong with me?"

It's changing us, Miri said yesterday on the beach.

"We have to go," I whisper. I rise and pull her to her feet.

"Where are all of our clothes?" Effie asks, clutching her slip to her chest.

"I don't know," I say. "C'mon. We need to get away from here."

I lead everyone out of the grove. We walk single-file except for Paris and Celia, who have their arms wrapped around each other.

I am mindful of each step. I choose the quietest path away from danger. I'm so focused on my feet that I'm not really paying attention to where we are going. Not until I see the wide trunk of the large tree right ahead of me. It is singularly massive, even in a forest of large trees. The moss is thickest here, and it feels ancient in a way the rest of the island does not.

I stop walking and Paris bumps into me.

There's a new kill on the tree.

This time it is the unmistakable skull of a large predator. A wolf, I think. Now it's nothing but teeth and bone and rotting flesh. Its yellow eyes are dull with decay. There is more than bone this time. At the base of the tree, lined in a row, are the animal's internal organs.

"Don't stop," Paris whispers behind me, gently nudging me forward.

We circle around the tree, and I want to turn back. I want to see if Vincent is still pinned to the other side, but I resist the urge.

I don't need to collect any new images to feed my nightmares.

Something crashes through the woods behind us, cracking branches off the bushes and startling some birds to flight. It could have been anything. A rabbit in the brush, or a dead branch breaking off a tree. But we don't wait to find out. We run.

In my head, I imagine our monster emerging from its watery den, dripping wet, stretching out those long claws for new prey.

I see a flash of blond hair to my left, and I reach for it. My hand finds Miri, and I grab on to her wrist, pulling her through the woods. The panic is so absolute, I'm not watching where we are going. I don't see the steep slope ahead of me until I am falling over it. I let go of Miri, but not soon enough, and she falls with me.

We roll several times. My hand reaches, trying to grab for something to stop my descent, and I snag a branch, but I'm falling too fast, and my hand rips along the wood, burning. It scrapes against the tip of my finger—the one I pricked, the one with the blooming growth—and I scream when I feel it ripped off me.

I land hard at the bottom of the ravine, all the air knocked from my lungs. I lie there for a long time, gaping like a fish. I panic, my chest heaving.

Finally, I gasp, sucking in a huge lungful of air.

I roll over. My forehead touches the hard ground and I try to calm my erratic breathing. There is a soft moan somewhere on the hill above me. I need to get up. Find Miri and the others.

My fingers clench on the ground for traction, but the earth doesn't give beneath them. I just leave a trail of blood from my shredded fingertip.

I open my eyes and look at my hand. Not at my mutilated finger, but what is below it. It isn't forest or dirt or sand at all. I scrape my nails against it, and finally lift my head to look around.

I fell onto a concrete slab.

To my right, there is more of it, built right into the side of the hill, so perfectly hiding the structure that we could have been stuck on this island for years and not found it.

It's a bunker.

"A bunker? Like a military bunker?" Rosa asks.

We've all gathered outside our strange discovery. It isn't very large, but it is distinctly man-made. There is even a door, though our first attempt to open it was humbling. We couldn't move it a centimeter, even with all of us pulling.

"We're somewhere in the Pacific Northwest," says Paris. "It's not that far-fetched to think the military might have had a station out here, to watch for Russian ships during the Cold War or something."

"I guess." Celia shrugs. "But how do we get in?"

"Now we could use Vincent's strength," Miri laments. Then her eyes went to her sister. "I'm sorry, Effie, I didn't mean—"

"No, screw that. We don't need him. We're going to get in there," Effie says, hand on her hip and head tilted like she is considering a math problem on a chalkboard, not a military bunker that had likely been sealed shut for decades.

I step to the door again and smack my fist on it. My good fist. My other hand is wrapped up in strips of cloth from my slip to stop my bleeding finger. It hurts like hell, and I'm afraid to look at it.

I run my fingers over the door for what must be the dozenth time, searching for some way in. There's no keyhole. No door handles. Nothing but a slight ridge on one side, and we could barely get our nails under it. We have no leverage to pull. The only reason we know it's a door is because of the massive hinges on one side of it.

The hinges.

I walk over to the other side of the door and bend down to the lower hinge. I brush the dirt off it, exposing the metal, and find exactly what I was hoping for. The hinge is rusted. It might be more fragile than the rest of the door because of exposure.

"What is it?" Paris asks, leaning over to look at what I am doing.

"I need a rock. Something kind of heavy."

There is some shuffling behind me, and then one of the girls passes a rock forward. It's slightly larger than my hand. I pull my good arm back and swing as hard as I can.

The rock shatters on impact, and my hand scrapes against the rusted metal.

"Dammit." I wait for the initial sharp shock of pain to subside before examining the damage I just did.

Two of my knuckles are shredded. I can see bits of my skin still caught on the sharp edge of the door hinge.

"Let me see," Miri says, still kneeling beside me. She draws my hand in tight, pulls it up to her mouth, and puts my bloody knuckles right between her lips. When she pulls back, I hear the wet sound of her mouth releasing my skin with a delicate pop.

"Sorry," she says. "I don't know why—"

"It's fine," I tell her. "Thank you." The stinging sharpness of the scrape across my knuckles is gone, replaced by a dull thud that keeps pace with my pulse.

Or maybe it matches Miri's pulse, instead.

Effie comes forward with a new rock, and I draw back and lean against Miri off to the side, happy to let someone else try.

I flinch with each strike of rock on metal. *Clink! Clink! Clink!* And then a louder sound, hollow and echoing, when the hinge gives out. It falls to the ground beneath the door, leaving a small hole in its place.

"You did it!" Miri cheers, unable to contain her excitement.

Effie, invigorated by her success, climbs the hill to reach the upper hinge. The angle is awkward, but this hinge is even more deteriorated than the first, and it only takes a few hard strikes of rock on the door to break it off as well. Effie slips her fingers into the hole up top, and Rosa grabs the one below.

"Be careful, the edges are really sharp," Effie says from above.

"I will. You ready?" Rosa asks.

They count together. *Three, two, pull.*

The door creaks. It groans. And then, like a miracle, it shifts outward.

"It's working," I say, climbing to my feet in excitement.

Rosa and Effie continue for a few more minutes, managing to wrench the door out a full inch, and then two. It takes time, and we trade off, with Miri and Celia taking over, and then Effie and Paris.

They let me and my two bloodied hands sit this one out.

It seems to take ages, and then, all at once, the door gives, shifting wide open like a gaping maw. There are stairs leading down into what feels like endless darkness. It seems none of us anticipated that, because no one volunteers to go first.

"We should go back to our camp for the lighter," I suggest. "We can make some kind of torch to take down with us."

"Good idea. I'll go," Effie says.

"In pairs," I say. "We don't know how we ended up in the woods last night. Whether that thing is moving around during the day or not. We should move in pairs."

"I'll go, too," Paris says.

They set off in the general direction of the shore.

"So what do you think?" Rosa asks, sitting down beside me. Her legs are stretched out in front of her, scaled leg glimmering in the sunlight flickering through the trees.

"I have no clue," I answer honestly. "Why did it move us all to the grove? Why didn't it hurt us like it hurt Vincent?"

"Maybe it didn't," Rosa says. "Maybe we went there ourselves."

"Like sleepwalking?"

Rosa nods. "We've all been having nightmares. Our bodies are hurting. It makes sense we are restless. Sleepwalking isn't that unbelievable."

"No, it's not," I agree, remembering the strange dreamlike state I was in when I followed the creature two nights ago. "But it's still really weird."

I laugh at Rosa's bluntness.

"Let me see that," she says, reaching for my hand. At first I think she means my bloody knuckles, but she reaches for my other arm.

"I haven't looked yet," I tell her.

"I'll look for you."

"It might be really bad," I say, and I explain to her what my finger looked like this morning when I woke up.

"Yeah, I have some experience in that area," Rosa says, pointing to her strange, transformed leg.

I turn away as Rosa unwraps my finger, and only turn back to look when she is quiet for a frustratingly long time. She's pinching my finger in her own, holding it up to examine it closer.

"It's healing already," she says. "Look."

I lean over to see what she means.

It's not as bad as I thought it would be. In fact, the injury looks weeks old instead of hours. But instead of my skin growing back over the wound the way it used to, it is growing up and out again. It's growing back into the strange, ribbed fungus shape that I found this morning.

"I guess that means I shouldn't try scraping off my scales," Rosa says.

"No, I don't think you should," I answer.

Whatever it is, it can't just be cut off. It's like it's part of us now.

"Rosa, can I ask you something?"

"Shoot," she says, still examining my strange finger.

"What happened last year? During the Olympics?"

I've wanted to ask her for ages. Ever since I stitched her little toe into place, and she told me about her broken ankle. But Rosa is like Effie. Independent. Distanced.

I realize I could be describing myself, too. Around everyone except Miri, that is.

But here we don't have a choice. We only have each other, and I want to know what happened to make one of the most talented gymnasts in the world have to walk away from it all.

"He lied," Rosa says simply. "I trusted my coach with my whole life. My career. My body. I landed on it wrong after the balance beam, and they rushed me back for an X-ray.

Coach cleared me. He said I would be fine. In a way he was right; I finished my routine. But I messed up my ankle real bad by performing on it like that."

Rosa wiggles her foot—the same one now covered in green scales.

"I had three surgeries in five months after that, but it never healed properly. The next time I tried to dismount, it broke again. They said my career was effectively over."

"All because of some asshole's ego?" I ask.

"Yep," Rosa confirms. "He dropped me in December. Told me he only coaches girls with Olympic potential."

"Did you report it?"

"We were working on it. Gathering statements from the physician who was there that day. Needed medical files, and the foundation's internal documents. But now . . ." Rosa shrugs. "I didn't even need it for me; it wouldn't change anything. But he shouldn't be allowed to coach."

"And then how did you end up on the yacht?" I ask.

"When I told Paris I was quitting gymnastics, she asked if I'd like to try acting. She'd just landed a lead in *The Tempest*, and they'd need some extras, and did I want to tag along. Get away from it all for a little bit. How could I say no? It's not like I had anything else going on."

"And now you are here," I conclude.

Rosa leans back on her arms, looking up at a patch of cloudy sky above us. It's overcast today, and the forest around us is in shadow. I don't think it's very warm, but Rosa and I are both sweaty, small beads of it rolling down our foreheads and chests.

"I don't know," Rosa says. "Maybe we all did something to deserve this. Fell into someone's bad graces."

"We didn't, Rosa. It was an accident."

Rosa shrugs. "I guess. But every day we spend here, I . . ." She stops talking, furrowing her brow. "Never mind."

"What is it?" I press.

Rosa looks up at me. "I don't completely hate it here," she says. "It feels like I'm free for the first time . . . well, ever. I don't have to be the best. I just get to live. I'm enough."

Enough.

I'd had almost the exact same thought not long ago. Our island might not be a utopia, but it was a safe haven of some kind, from a world that had already knocked us down and told us to stay there. *We're teenage girls,* Effie said on our first day on the island. *We've all been prey before.*

But the others were all escaping pressure that had been crushing them in the real world, whereas I would have given anything to have some expectations set on me. Expectations meant potential. They meant someone at least cared enough to ask more of you. Instead, I knew intimately how it felt to just be forgotten. Not even worth a resting place in a memory.

There is a version of me that was cherished and I think about her all the time. What would she be like? What could she have done? But she's blurry in my mind, faceless. A girl I don't know—at least, not before this place.

When Effie and Paris return, Paris patches up my knuckles with a bit of antibiotic cream, even though what I really need is a tetanus booster. We don't bother to wrap them—I need to be able to use my hands, and the bleeding has mostly stopped. She's also packed up sweatshirts and distributes them.

Three of us opt to stay in only the slips. The three of us who have been injured on the island, changed by it. The three of us with what seems to be permanent changes to our fingers, arms, feet, ears. Permanent flushes on our cheeks. Near-constant sheens of sweat on our warm bodies.

We are all aware of it, but we don't discuss it. We have no idea what it means.

"Ready?" Effie asks.

She stands a head taller than the rest of us, holding a torch made of some branches and strips of cloth, meshed with some dry leaves and what I think might be strands of hair from one of the wigs.

No, they're auburn. Effie plucked them from her head.

She lights the torch and leads the way. We file into the dark stairwell behind her. It isn't far to the bottom, only ten or twelve steps, and then our feet hit the earthen floor at the base of the bunker. Effie moves ahead, one arm outstretched, letting the dim, flickering light reach as far as it can.

There are stacked metal crates lining the bunker, and I move to the nearest box and open it. "Blankets," I say, lifting one. It's scratchy but dry, and when I unfold it, it's thick, maybe wool, and there are more underneath.

Paris pulls the lid off another crate beside mine. "Matches," she says, sliding a small box open to reveal the prize inside. She reaches down and pulls out a small metal container, unscrewing the top.

She starts to cough, and I take the bottle from her, holding it farther away this time.

"What is it?" I ask.

"That's kerosene," Celia says. "I can smell it from here. We used to light our lamps with it for campouts."

I reach farther into the crate Paris opened and find exactly what I'd hoped would be in there.

"A lantern," Celia says, stepping forward. She unscrews part of the lantern and takes the metal canister from me, pouring the kerosene in. "Let's see if it's any good, right?"

She strikes a match and holds it to the small wick inside the lantern.

But the match only sizzles out, again and again.

"It's too degraded, I think," Celia says.

We follow Effie's light across the bunker. She's stopped moving and her hand is shaking slightly, causing the quickly fading light to shimmer and dance across the walls of the small room. We reach her side, and I see what Effie has stopped to stare at.

There is a skeleton propped against the wall, bones bare beneath the military-green uniform it is wearing.

The skeleton is . . . all wrong. The jaw is misaligned and protruding farther than a human jaw ought to. The eye sockets are too large. And the skull—the skull is blown open in the back, with remnants of old fungi extending out in every direction, deadened gray tendrils creeping across the concrete side of the bunker. It's like the mushrooms burst out of his head.

I hope he was already dead when it happened.

Above the skeleton, carved into the wall by what might have been fingernails if the bloody streaks around the letters were any indication, are two words.

DISCO INFERNO.

Effie's torch burns out, pitching us into darkness.

21

DISCO INFERNO.

The darkness is absolute in a way that nothing else on the island has been. There has always been moonlight, or the stars, or at least the comfort of a burning fire. Even last night, we slept beneath the shine of the creature's lair.

But inside the bunker, there is nothing. My heart begins to punch inside my chest. I silently berate myself for my ridiculous fear. There is a literal monster here. I've been within inches of it. Yet it's still the darkness I hate most.

Then again, in my defense, it isn't only the dark this time.

It is the dark of an abandoned military bunker buried underground, deep in the woods of a strange island, in the company of a mutilated skeleton that's been sealed in here for decades, belonging to someone who carved his final words into a concrete wall.

Maybe this time my fear is justified.

I feel Miri slip her hand into mine, and suddenly it's a little more bearable.

"Disco inferno." I repeat the words I read before the torch went out. "What does it mean?"

"*Disco* is . . . 'I am learning,'" Celia says in the dark. "*Inferno* could mean hell, or suffering. So it might be 'I am learning about hell' or 'I am learning through suffering,' or something similar to those."

"How on earth do you know that?" Rosa asks.

"Twelve years of school at Our Mother of Eternal Sorrow, my all-girls Catholic prep school, thank you very much. And this is the first time it's ever been of any practical use to me. Our school motto was *Video, Audio, Disco.* 'I see, I hear, I learn.'"

"You're joking," I say.

"Don't ever say nuns don't have a wicked sense of humor," Celia says seriously.

"Hey, let's get the hell out of here," Paris says, straining her voice to talk to us from the far end of the room. "It's giving me the heebie-jeebies in the dark."

"Fair," Miri says. "But everyone should grab a crate on the way out—we'll do some inventory outside where we can see."

"What about . . . him?" Effie asks, and I assume she's referring to our long-dead companion against the wall.

"We'll figure it out later," Celia says. "For now, let's see if there's anything useful in here."

We spread out on the concrete just outside of the bunker to sort through the contents of the crates. There are about a dozen of them altogether, and the task of organizing takes us well into the afternoon. We find a toolbox that contains a hammer, a saw, and a small container of nails and screws. Rosa finds a carton of cigarettes but opens them to find more bright blue mushrooms.

"Unless you want your lungs to look like my shoulder, you should probably toss those," I say.

There are even a few large bottles of whiskey.

Effie unscrews one, and the *crack-split* of the seal breaking tells us it's probably good even before she takes a swig of the alcohol. "God bless the Irish," she says, holding up the bottle to read the worn label.

"We need to save that," I tell her. "It'll fuel fires. Clean wounds."

"It'll let us drink ourselves into a warm stupor when we run out of food," Celia adds dryly.

"Hey, check these out," I say, lifting items from the bottom of my last crate. "What are they? Flashlights?"

They are military green, with the words *DACO-LITE* stamped on one side, and the words *Dayton Acme Co. Cincinnati Ohio* stamped on the other. I squeeze the handle against the box—it's some kind of hand-powered energy—and I'm rewarded when the light bulb glows dimly inside the glass.

"Better than nothing," Rosa says, picking up another flashlight and turning the light on and off a few times to test it.

In the last crate I find a small shovel, more blankets, and

six sheathed items. I unbutton one of the leather covers and slide it off to find gleaming metal underneath.

"They're knives," I tell the others, holding one up. It catches the sunlight and reflects the gleam into Effie's eyes. "Sorry," I say, dropping the blade down.

"We should each carry one." Rosa steps forward to take the knives. She checks all of them, and they're in good condition except for a few spots of rust. "For self-defense."

Miri has one of my notebooks and is making a list of everything from the bunker.

"It isn't a lot," she says to me without looking up, like she felt me reading over her shoulder. "The shelter itself is the most valuable thing. Especially if we are stuck here a while longer."

It was early August when we wrecked, and it's still warm during the day on the island. I haven't been keeping track of the days. At first I was too optimistic to count them. It wouldn't matter because we'd be rescued right away. And then as time went on, the inverse became true. It was too depressing to tick off the days, knowing that with each one that passed, our chances of rescue became less likely.

Miri is referring to being here when it's cold, months from now, when this shelter will be the only thing keeping us alive. Although by then the weather won't matter so much, because our primary food sources will be gone. Figs and fish will be scarce when the season turns. And then Celia's morbid prophecy will become real. All we will have left is the whiskey.

"You really don't think they'll find us?" I ask. "They must be searching."

"In the wrong place, remember?" Miri says. She starts to make a neat stack of blankets from one of the crates. "The navigation was down. We weren't where we were supposed to be. Vincent practically ensured disaster."

"They'll keep broadening their search," Rosa argues. "Hopefully our island will fall inside one of those perimeters eventually."

None of us says anything in response to that. There isn't anything to say when your entire life hinges on the word *hopefully*.

We take a break to track down some of the fig bushes to quench our hunger and our thirst. We let the juice of the fruit drip down our chins without caring about the mess. Afterward, Rosa takes a flashlight and ventures back down into the bunker to make sure we didn't miss any crates. She emerges carrying one last thing. It's large as a backpack, and the same military green as the flashlights.

"Look what Lionel had next to him," she says, setting it down on the ground.

"Lionel?" Miri asks.

"The skeleton. It said Corporal L. Hamm on the shoulder

of his military jacket." Rosa shrugs. "He looks like a Lionel to me."

"He's a skeleton," Celia says. "He doesn't look like anything except mushroom food. No offense." Celia directs the last bit at me, and I frown at the implication.

"Excuse me, I'm not mushroom *food*," I tell her, holding up my arm. "I am the mushroom itself. The mushroom and I are one."

Celia kneels at the backpack and starts messing with the knobs. "Well, it's ancient, but I think this is a radio system."

"Really?" I ask, sitting forward. "Could you fix it?"

"Even if I can, I doubt there's anyone near enough to receive a signal from this. But I'll give it a shot."

Celia digs the nail clippers out of my backpack and uses the file to undo the screws along the side of the radio. It's caked in dirt, but she finally loosens the last one, and the backpack starts to split open along the seam on its side.

"Oh, my god, ew!" Celia shouts, leaping to her feet.

"What!" I am sitting right behind her, and I crawl away on my hands and knees. "What is it?"

"Oh, yuck," Celia says, running her hands up and down her body in revulsion. "Something moved. Something . . . wriggled."

I kick at the pack, flipping it open. I breathe a sigh of relief.

"It's a snake, Celia." I reach down and pick it up, letting it curl around my fingers. "See? Harmless."

"Liv, what the hell are you doing?" Rosa asks. "It could bite you."

"It's not dangerous. It's a ring-necked snake."

I repeat the same words that were said to me, last summer, when the same kind of snake slithered into my tent when I went camping with Everly. She'd come running when I screamed, and caught the snake, showing me with her hands that it was safe, turning it over to show me the bright orange-red of its belly.

She's more scared of you, Liv.

Doubt that, I'd told her, but I took the snake from her when she offered it. We walked it to the edge of the woods together. *You're more intimidating than you know,* Everly had said as we watched the snake slip away into the shadows.

"To be clear," Celia says, stepping forward and taking the snake from me, "I'm not scared of snakes. It's *surprise* snakes that I have a problem with."

"Gross," Miri says, peering into the inner parts of the radio. "I think it broke your radio, Cel."

The inside of it is filled with the snake's shed and the fur and bones of creatures it couldn't fully digest.

I spy Paris sitting off to the side, her arms draped around her bent knees, head tilted ever so slightly to the side, like she's listening to something far away. I go sit beside her, bringing the little snake with me.

"How are *you* feeling?" I ask her.

Paris leans her head on my shoulder.

"Weird." Her voice is still a scratchy whisper. "No voice. Impeccable hearing. There is a mouse crawling on the steps of the bunker right now. And a baby bird eating worms from its mother in that tree right there." She nods toward the nearest pine tree. "I can hear your heart beating. And everyone else's, for that matter. Even the snake's heart."

Paris reaches for the snake. It moves back and forth between us, tickling against my skin as it slides past the mushrooms on my arm.

"It probably thinks you're a tree branch," Paris says, and I shove at her playfully.

We let the snake go, watch it slither into the mossy undergrowth beside us.

Effie stands up, brushing off her sides and looking like she's decided something.

"Okay, now that everything is counted," Effie says, "I think we should move in here."

"Into the bunker?" Miri asks, her tone doing nothing to hide her dislike of the idea. "No way. It's creepy as hell, Ef."

"Creepy, sure. But it's safe. We don't know what happened last night. How we wound up in the woods. There's something strange in that grove, and I think we will be safer here."

"What about Lionel?" Rosa asks. "Should we really disturb his resting place?"

"Lionel can stay," Effie says.

Miri shudders but doesn't argue it further. It's not ideal, but Effie is right. We ought to move to the bunker.

We break into two groups. Paris, Rosa, and I agree to move the crates back into the bunker and organize things. The others head to the beach to gather our belongings.

We've just barely finished moving everything into the bunker at dusk. We're all hungry, having only eaten a few figs all day. But none of us has the energy to try for a fish or a fire, and it's too late anyway, with night falling. The creature could come for us again tonight.

We go to bed hungry, curling on our cushions with our scratchy military blankets over us.

I hate the feel of it, and I'm burning up anyway, so I kick it off me.

With the outer door pulled shut, the dark is absolute. I've become so used to us all sleeping in the small shelter on the rocky beach, our bodies pressed tight together to fit into the small space. I miss the stars at night above me, and the others touching me. Even when it was too hot, it was comforting. I miss the crashing of waves lulling me to sleep, a distraction from the constant hunger echoing inside of me.

Tonight, I feel only longing, and it is earnest and acute. An emptiness that is more than my growling stomach. After a lifetime of being fine on my own, I've grown accustomed to being very near to the other girls on this island, night and day.

It's strange how quickly my awareness of time has changed.

With no phone or watch to track it, I've relied on the sun or stars for some sense of shifting hours. Down here, that's gone, too. So it might be only one hour, or maybe it's three or four, but I lie in the dark for a long time, until the sound of breathing all around me becomes slow and regular with sleep.

Then I hear someone shifting in the dark.

One of the makeshift beds is slid right next to mine, and a warm body—almost uncomfortably warm against my own feverish skin—presses against my back. An arm wraps around my middle, just like she did in the woods after I screamed at the wolf.

Miri.

I reach for her arm around my waist and loop our fingers together, knuckles squeezing just on the verge of too tight. I realize what a gift it is for someone to know your needs and meet you there, without even having to ask. Without being made to feel like a burden.

I no longer feel like I could fly to pieces, lost forever in the nothingness around me like a star falling into a black hole. In Miri's arms, I feel safe.

When we emerge from the bunker the next day, the sun is high in the sky.

"Wow. We slept in." Paris still hasn't gotten her voice back. Her voice is no more than a hoarse whisper behind me as we climb the stairs.

"We needed it," I say. We'd been up with the sunrise every morning since we washed ashore. We'd spent every day on our feet, gathering supplies, fishing, swimming out to the wreck, and with limited food for energy. We were all exhausted.

Even after more than a full night of sleep, we still have purple shadows under our eyes. And yet we are better rested now than we have been since we wrecked here, and I can't deny how good it feels. How hopeful it makes me.

"I'll find some breakfast," Effie offers. That means more figs, the only thing safe to consume beyond the fish.

"Hey, look at this," Rosa says. She's holding a green leather book, flipping through the pages. "It was in Lionel's jacket pocket."

I lean over Rosa's shoulder to read. "It's some kind of log," I realize, scanning the dates and entries.

When Effie returns with the fruit, we sit on the concrete just outside the bunker to eat it, and Rosa reads aloud from the book. We were right about the bunker. It was built during the Second World War to try to intercept communications, but it was quickly abandoned. And then four soldiers were dropped here during the Cold War.

"It says they were meant to be here a year, to watch for warships," Rosa says. "But it looks like none of their comms ever worked, even from the first day."

"Didn't someone come back for them?" I ask, wiping fig juice off my lips. It's overripe, dripping sticky-sweet nectar.

"If they did, they wouldn't have found them alive," Rosa says. *"September eighteenth. We've managed to set up a comms tower on the highest point of the island. No signals received."*

"A tower?" Celia perks up. "It might still be there."

"It says right there it didn't work," Miri points out.

"Worth finding it," Celia says. "The parts might be useful."

"Keep reading," I encourage Rosa. She's been scanning the text while they talk, her eyes growing more concerned as she read. She climbs to her feet and paces as she continues.

"October ninth. Colonel Roberts never returned to base camp last night. Our team departed from our bunker at 21:00 hours

to search for him. His remains were found on the southern point of the island. Cause of death is unclear, but the violence and dismemberment indicate a very large predator of some kind."

"It was her," Miri says. "The monster. You know, I'm thinking we should just give her some kind of name. Calling her 'the monster' makes her seem so . . ."

"Terrifying? Like she is?" I ask.

"We don't know that it was her," Effie says.

Rosa turns another page. *"October twentieth. Concerned about the mental health of Lieutenant Bates. Claims to have seen the predator responsible for the death of Roberts. Described a woman with long green hair, black claws, and no face."*

No face.

I remember kneeling in the pool. The flash of brilliant blue-white light as I raised my head to look at her, and then—

And then nothing. I never saw her face. Or if I did, I have no recollection of it.

"What else, Rosa?" I ask.

"Last entry is dated October thirty-first. *The others are gone. Roberts and Bates were killed by whatever haunts this island. Hanson died of some kind of illness three days ago. I believe I have it, too. My head throbs with even the slightest movement. I can no longer gather drinking water. I'm sure I'll die in this place.*

"That's it. That's all there is." Rosa stops pacing.

"How long did they survive here?" Celia asks.

Rosa flips back to the first entry. "Starts mid-September. So, maybe six weeks."

"It was *her*," Miri says again. "And the soldiers changed, just like we are now."

"Enough, Miri," Effie snaps, her mounting frustration etched in the frown across her face. "You are just guessing. We have no idea what really happened to them."

"I'm sorry, but did you somehow miss the skeleton with exploding mushroom brains down there?" Miri shouts.

"Celia, please back me up on this," Effie says. "Tell Miri that there are perfectly reasonable explanations for what we've seen here."

Celia's eyes go wide when she's put on the spot between the two Knight sisters.

"Of course there are," Celia says.

Effie raises her eyebrows into perfect auburn arches, her satisfaction gracing her lips.

"But I haven't the slightest idea what they could be," Celia adds.

"She thinks it's like a fairy tale, Celia. Magic. Monsters," Effie argues.

"And we once believed a chariot drawn by celestial horses pulled the sun across the sky each day," Celia says. "It's all magic, Effie, until it's not. And we don't always get the explanations we want."

Effie throws her arms up in defeat and heads into the woods.

"Effie, you said we shouldn't wander off alone," Rosa calls after her.

"I'm not wandering," she calls back over her shoulder. "I'm deliberately walking away. I'll collect firewood. Or do something *really* useful, like dance naked under a full moon."

Once Effie's angry footsteps fade into the sounds of the forest, Celia looks around. "So, someone should probably go after her, right?"

We all look to Miri. She is still scowling in the direction her sister went. She turns back and finds four pairs of eyes judging her.

"Oh, for the love of—fine. I'll get her." Miri rolls her eyes and starts to walk toward the forest. She stops at the edge and turns back again, indignation scrawled into every expressive feature of her perfect, petulant face. "Liv!"

"Oh, right. Okay." I climb to my feet and hurry to catch up with her.

As soon as I'm by her side, Miri slips her hand into mine like that's the obvious place for it. Like we are a habit.

"She's mad because she feels guilty," Miri says without me prompting her. I'm not sure we are even really looking for Effie. Our pace is too slow. Almost leisurely.

"Why guilty?" I ask. I run my thumb over the fleshy part of Miri's hand. I didn't know physical touch was a thing you could hunger for, but I feel it now. I want to touch her. I want her to put her arms around me like she did last night. I want to sink into more kisses, longer kisses. I want specifically to kiss the curved line of freckles just above her collarbone. Three of them, like Orion's Belt.

I've missed whatever Miri just said.

"Sorry, what?" I ask again, my cheeks heating at the direction my mind was veering.

Miri gives me that Clark Kent stare. The one where it feels like she sees right through me. Reads all my thoughts and secrets.

"I *said* that if she hadn't been with Vincent, we'd never have been on his godforsaken yacht in the first place. She feels guilty we're here. That's why she's fighting my theories so hard."

"Your theories?" I laugh.

"Yes. *Theories*. I might not practice the full scientific method like Celia or deduce things quite as well as Sherlock Holmes, but it seems obvious to me that something preternatural is going on. People's brains don't just explode from their skulls. Monsters aren't supposed to be real. And fingers don't turn into mushrooms."

Miri lifts my mutilated hand in evidence.

"It's like we've slipped into a Greek myth," she says. "Banished to an island, like Circe. We are being punished by the gods."

"Punished for what?" I ask.

"For being too pretty," she quips without hesitation.

I burst out laughing. "Thank god your *ego* hasn't suffered

any calamities out here." I stop walking and tug Miri back to me. She turns in my arm and there is no hesitation at all, no self-consciousness, before we press our lips together. Hers are cool to the touch, and mine are fevered. My fingers tangle in her hair. Her nails press into the skin on my arms.

When she breaks the kiss to suck in air, I kiss the little soft hollow beneath her ear. Her skin tastes like the ocean, and she smells sweet like the figs.

"Seriously? Again?"

Celia stands a few yards away. This time it isn't a knowing smirk she gives us, but a wide grin. "You two are worse than us."

"Celia Jones, I will murder you," Miri says. She stomps her foot for good measure. I won't tell her how adorable that is. But I can't stop myself from thinking it.

"Listen, I was sent to recover you. Effie is back. She wants a few of us to go look for the communications tower."

"We'll go!" Miri volunteers us, lifting my hand for me.

"We will?" I ask.

Celia frowns. "Well, all right, I guess that solves it. We thought we'd have to draw straws or something. No one else wants to hike up there."

Celia nods to some area behind us, and Miri and I turn to look at the high peak of the island. It's thick with trees up there—we'd tried to go up once before and had to turn back. It wasn't walkable.

"We volunteer?" I ask her once Celia turns back for the bunker.

"We do," Miri says. "Look up there. Do you see that?"

I stare at the hill.

"No? There's nothing up there."

"Exactly," she says. "We will actually have some privacy up there."

"That's why you volunteered us to climb a nearly vertical incline through dense foliage to search for a decades-old rusty comms tower? For privacy?"

"Obviously," Miri says.

"How romantic," I say, and pretend to faint, throwing my arm across my forehead in faux theatrics.

Miri catches my fall.

"Maybe leave the dramatics to me," she says. "You aren't a very believable swooner."

"Fair enough."

"Say you'll go with me," Miri says. "Please."

I'm not sure Miri is my first choice of partner for trekking up a massive, steep incline. She's going to whine the whole way up. But there's no one else I want to kiss at the top.

"Okay," I acquiesce. "We'll go."

"Swear it," she demands, stepping closer, and when the light catches the gold speckles in her green eyes, I realize I was never going to refuse.

"Cross my heart."

* * *

We return to the bunker to gather some items. I fill my backpack with full water bottles and some fruit. While we looked for Effie, Paris and Rosa managed to catch another salmon in the creek. We help cook it and then wrap a few portions to take with us to eat later. Miri and I each take one of the hunting knives, tying them around our waists.

"We'll try to hurry back," I say.

"Sun sets in about six hours," Effie reminds us.

"We'll be back long before then," Miri promises as we set off.

But we aren't.

By the time we've climbed about halfway up, the sun has begun its descent.

The ground is rockier up here, and our climb is slow as we try not to twist our ankles. There are fewer pine trees and more tall, leafy ones, with roots as thick as our legs erupting from the ground.

There are mammals of some kind scrambling around in the rocks. Weasels, perhaps. Or marmots. My mouth waters when I wonder what they taste like.

When the canopy breaks above us, I take the opportunity to check the position of the sun.

"We need to turn back," I tell Miri, "or we won't make it by nightfall."

Miri looks back the way we came, wearing defeat across

her face like she's waving a white flag. "Oh, screw that. I'm not doing this a second time."

"Then what do you propose we do?" I pull one of the waters from my bag and lean against a tree while I drink it.

"We spend the night up there," Miri says.

I bark my laughter. "Are you out of your mind? Did you forget the ravenous monster? The one that has no trouble at all tearing apart grown men?"

"I didn't forget," Miri says. "But we might need whatever is up there. And this is our best shot. We've made it this far, Liv. Let's finish what we came to do."

"Fine," I concede. "But if the monster finds us, she gets to eat you first."

"Deal."

We reach the summit as the first golden-pink streaks of sunset appear in the sky above us. We've only barely made it before nightfall, and there is nothing even remotely like a shelter up here. We will have to sleep out in the open, exposed. Vulnerable.

"Look," Miri says, pulling grass and moss off a metal lattice frame on the ground. "It's the tower. Shouldn't there be . . . a lot more here? Like a base for it?"

We both look down at the same moment. Anything else must be buried by years of dirt and dust and weather. I sigh and pull out the small shovel we recovered from the bunker, though I'd hoped we wouldn't need it. Miri and I take turns digging around the tower, uncovering its base as best we can, searching for anything that might be of use.

By the time it starts to grow dark, we've only found an ancient can opener and a rusted belt buckle. We are parched, hungry, and every muscle aches from digging when we finally call it.

There's nothing up here for us.

I pull the last of our food from my bag, handing some fruit and fish to Miri. We split one water bottle and save the other two for the morning hike back down.

From up here, the ocean feels infinite around us. In every direction, as far as we can see, there is only water.

When we finish eating, we lie on the grass and watch the sky shift from twilight to dusk to the inky black of a fathomless night. It's like someone's knocked over a cup of honey and stars, the way they slowly seep across the sky above us.

I listen for the creature, but I don't hear anything to cause alarm. Crickets chirp nearby. Something small, maybe a mouse or a vole, scurries across the metal frame of the tower, its tiny feet scratching against it.

Miri scoots closer, curling her cool body against mine. Her lips find mine in the dark, followed quickly by hands. I feel like we are great explorers, navigating uncharted territory. We catch summit fever, compelled to reach some unknown peak together. I didn't know it was possible to drown in someone, or how much I would love it. But I think maybe kissing Miri is more important to my survival out here than breathing is.

"*Oh, brave new world, that has such people in it,*" Miri whispers against my skin when we finally break apart for air.

"Did you seriously just quote Shakespeare?" I whisper back.

"Of course I did," she says. "The moment called for it."

"So pretentious," I say, smiling despite myself.

I'm starting to drift off to sleep when Miri gasps beside me, startling me awake. Her green eyes are wide.

"What is it?" I reach for the hunting knife at my hip.

"Look," she sighs, pointing straight up.

I crane my neck to follow her outstretched arm. Lights shimmer in the sky all around us, shifting waves of blue-green and violet. It's the northern lights.

"Oh."

It is all I can say, because for the first time in my life, I feel genuine awe. The kind that makes me feel so small in the universe, and so lucky to be alive. Even here. My fingers find Miri's in the dirt.

Especially here.

"Isn't it the most beautiful thing you've ever seen?" I ask.

"So far," Miri says quietly. "Do you think we're going to die here?" There's no sadness in her voice, only curiosity.

"I don't know," I answer honestly. "But I can think of worse places to die."

Like pressed under a scratchy pillow in a strange home

by your own sister, slowly suffocating.

"Like in a shark's mouth," Miri says. "That would hurt."

"Or falling into lava."

"Floating out into the depths of space all alone."

"Yeah, that's the worst," I agree. Before this place, I'm not sure that idea would have bothered me so much. Being alone was what I knew best. Even my own sister didn't want me. At least I'd have the stars. A great view till the very end. But now, the idea of it sends fear through me with a jolt. "You'd watch Earth get smaller and smaller. Every moment is the closest you'll ever be to another human being, ever again."

"Morbid, Liv."

"You started it."

"Well, the odds aren't really in our favor. They'll call off the searches soon, if they haven't already. So we probably will die here, eventually. But we get to live here first."

We are quiet for a few moments, lost in thought about our impending doom.

"Are you scared?" she asks.

"No," I answer immediately.

"You're a liar, Liv Whitlock." It's not the first time she says it, and I'm sure it won't be the last. Because I am a liar.

"Do you think people can change?" I ask.

I want her to say yes so badly. I want her to believe that I am more than *volatile, occasionally violent Violet*. But I'm not sure if I've changed. I don't know what parts of me are real and what parts were born out of necessity, to survive what I grew up in.

"Like this?" she asks, lifting my hand against the night sky. My finger ends in twists and curves that are already becoming familiar to me. I can't remember what it used to feel like.

"No," I tell her. "Like real change, like down to your very core."

"Well . . ." Miri trails off. She's thoughtful, watching the dancing lights above us while she forms her answer. "I think that's the wrong question, Liv."

"What's the right one?"

"The question is: Can people stay the same?" she tells me. "We are still just animals. We're all growing, learning, adapting to our environment. I don't think we can help it. We evolve."

"Effie is going to actually kill us," Miri says as we make the long trek back down the hill the next morning.

"At least then she'd know exactly where we are at all times. Right where she buried us."

It's a cool day, and we're grateful for it as we walk. There are storms rolling across the ocean, maybe heading this way. It hasn't rained on the island since we wrecked here, and I kind of hope one reaches us. A shower in the rain would be refreshing after having only saltwater baths in the sea and rinsing our clothes in the shallows of the creek.

"Can I admit that I'm a little glad there was nothing up there?" I confess.

"Why's that?" Miri says.

"Because if there was, they'd make us go back up there to fix it, or worse, carry it all down. And I am never doing that climb again."

"Me neither," she huffs. We're both out of breath.

I step into a low-hanging branch, pushing it out of our way and knocking something soft and brown off it. It implodes with a puff of air when it hits the ground.

A thousand tiny bugs start to pour out of it.

They cover my feet in an instant, climbing up my bare legs. I start swiping them off me, but they're so fast. There are so many of them. I trip over my own feet in my panic, and when I get up again, they're covering my arms.

I can't stand it. They're all over me. A sob escapes my throat.

And then Miri is there, her hands holding me still.

"Stop moving, I'm here. I can do it," she says, and she begins to brush the bugs off me. "Take off your clothes," she says.

I pull off my shirt and shorts, and stand there, half-naked, with my arms crossed over my sports bra.

Miri shakes the bugs off my clothes. She's systematic, turning the fabric inside out and then the pockets of my shorts.

"Thank god," she says. "I was starting to think you weren't scared of anything after the snake. But here we have it. Evidence that you are, in fact, just as human as the rest of us."

"I really, really don't like bugs. Especially bugs that *swarm*." Just saying the word makes me gag a little.

"I gathered that much," Miri says, handing my clothes back to me.

"Can you . . . can you please check my hair for them?" I

ask once I'm dressed.

"Sure," she says.

I sit down on a tree trunk nearby.

"Oh, right now?"

"Yes. Please. Right now."

Miri stands behind me, slowly detangling my hair, sectioning it, and carefully checking for any remaining critters.

"Can I ask why?"

"There was a head-lice infestation in one of my foster homes," I explain to her. "It was awful. The school sent notices home, so all the other kids knew I had them and made fun. My foster mom didn't really do anything about it, so it just went on and on. My scalp itched all the time, and I'd scratch and scratch until it was always bleeding and covered in sores. Eventually, I got so desperate to stop it that I cut all my hair off with kitchen scissors. . . . Sorry, you must be so grossed out."

"You're good," Miri says. "No bugs."

I stand up and face her. "Thank you. Really, thank you."

"I'm not grossed out, Liv."

"You're not?"

"No. I'm sad. And angry. And I wish I could go back in time and protect little Liv from a very unkind world."

"Well, you're protecting her now," I say.

Miri takes my hand, the one with the little morel sprouts made of veins growing out of my finger. There are folds of bluish-gray skin, and Miri's fingers trace over them gently, memorizing the new topography of my skin. The mycology of me.

She lifts my hand and kisses it.

Our joy is short-lived, however, because within a half hour we make it back to the bunker and the wrath of Ophelia Knight.

"The most irresponsible, asinine, *childish* . . ."

"We didn't mean to—"

"I'm not done," Effie says, whirling on me.

Eventually, the others make a meal and bring food to Miri and me, sitting down to watch the Effie show with us.

At one point Paris leans over and whispers in my ear.

"I was right, wasn't I?"

"About what?" I whisper when Effie's back is turned. She's explaining to Miri that she went through all the stages of grief last night.

"It kind of *was* worth dying for, right?" she says, and winks at me.

Heat burns across my face when I recall what she said after she and Celia snuck off together for privacy.

"Right?" She nudges me, and I know I'm not getting out of it.

"Yes," I admit, aware that I am blushing furiously.

Paris squeals and throws her arms around me.

"What?" Effie asks, turning on us.

"I'm just so glad they're back safe and sound," Paris says.

Effie eventually ends her tirade, and I remember what Miri said about Effie's temper before. She thought her sister felt guilty, but I think it's more than that. Effie doesn't just want to keep Miri safe, she *needs* to, because it's the only way the world makes sense. If she can just know that her sister is okay, if she can just do this one thing right, then all the other hurts and harms will have been worth it. She protected the thing that mattered most.

Miri might not ever understand Effie. But I do.

"Liv, wake up."

For a moment I am back on the *Bianca* before it capsized. I wonder if all our time on the island is one long, strange dream. I'm surprised by the hollow feeling of loss that hits me at the thought.

When I open my eyes, it isn't the soft ocean glow on the ceiling of my room on the boat, but the deep darkness of the bunker that greets me.

"Liv, wake up. They're gone." It's Paris shaking me awake, her voice still thick with sleep.

"I'm awake. What's going on?" I ask.

Paris has one of the flashlights, and I follow its circle of yellow light bouncing around the bunker. It falls on Rosa and Effie first, who are just now sitting up at the noise we are making. The light falls on Miri's pallet next, pressed up beside mine.

Only now it's empty.

Then it finds the one that Celia and Paris had fallen asleep on together.

Celia is gone, too.

"Miri?" Effie calls out. There's no answer.

Effie grabs the flashlight from Paris and shines it all around the bunker, into every corner and behind the stack of crates we organized just a few hours ago.

"Miri!" Effie's voice has real fear in it now. "Celia!"

"Shh," Paris says. "Listen."

We fall silent, and finally the rest of us can hear what Paris was already attuned to: crickets, and the breeze in the trees, rustling leaves.

"The door is open," I realize.

The four of us charge for the stairs that lead up and out into darkness. It is still night. I have no idea how long I was asleep for. I don't know how Miri and Celia left without waking any of us, especially Paris.

I take off into the forest without hesitation, not caring when branches crack beneath my feet. "Miri!" I scream, my voice echoing through the dark woods.

"Liv!" Effie catches up, grabs my arm. "You can't. It will hear you."

"I don't care." I wrench free of her grip and feel her nails scrape some of the lichen off my forearm. She's right. I know she's right. We both saw what it did to Vincent, and the wolf.

"I'm scared, too," Effie says, her voice gentler this time.

"We're going to find them. But we have to be careful."

I'm breathing too fast, with a sob caught like a hook in my chest.

"I promise, Liv."

"Listen," Paris whispers. "Everyone quiet so I can listen."

We stand there for so long I want to scream.

Anything could be happening to them right now.

"That way," Paris croaks, pointing south.

We move as a group this time, with me and Effie in front and Rosa and Paris right behind us. Every few minutes, Paris makes us pause so she can listen, and then we set off again in whatever direction she points. We try to move quickly, but without making unnecessary noise.

"Stop!" Paris whispers suddenly. "This is it."

We stand still in the darkness, and the roaring of blood in my ears quiets. I hear it, too.

There is a whimper from somewhere above us. We all crane our necks to look up. Most of the trees on the island are large, but the one beside us is singularly huge. I take a step back and realize which tree it is. My breath catches in my chest.

A white glimmer against the dark green moss of the trunk confirms my fear. There are more bones on it tonight, though I can't make out what kind of animal it is in the dark. Another sound from high in the branches draws my attention back up.

"Someone is up there," I say. I reach for the lowest branch of the tree, but it's still a few feet out of reach for me. "Can someone give me a boost?"

"Are you sure?" Rosa asks.

"Yeah, but hurry, we don't know where—" A cracking branch interrupts me, and we all stop moving.

For a full minute there isn't even a gentle whisper of breath among us as we wait. But nothing emerges from the trees around us.

"Hurry," I whisper, reaching again for the branch.

The others surge forward, with Effie putting her hands down into a sling for me to step into, and Paris and Rosa letting me push off their shoulders.

I grasp the lowest branch, barely trusting it with my weight, and pull myself up.

I climb as fast as I can on the slick branches. The entire tree is covered in moss and the blue-violet mushrooms that grow everywhere on the island. I smash them as I climb, and my hands slip a few times. I dig my nails into the bark as hard as I can for grip.

I don't know what I'm looking for beyond some instinct that tells me to hurry up and get there. That whimper felt too familiar, too distinctly girlish, and I'm sure it's one of them.

I'm halfway up when I see it. There is a massive nest in the branches above—larger than any I've ever seen before. We've watched the eagles come and go from the island, but

I hadn't seen any of their nests before now.

I'm stricken with doubt. Maybe it was just an eagle we heard. Their cries could almost sound human. But I keep climbing, driven only by a gut feeling.

Finally, my fingers touch the roughly woven branches of the bottom of the nest. I have to maneuver around the trunk, stepping across the branches slowly and ensuring they can hold me before giving them my full weight. The branches are thinner this high up.

I pull myself up a few more inches, and peer into the nest.

It's Miri.

She's curled in a tight ball, arms wrapped around herself.

She's wearing only the slip again.

"Miri," I say, reaching for her. She whimpers again, like before, but doesn't wake. She's dreaming. I think she must have been sleepwalking. It's a miracle she didn't fall to her death already.

My balance shifts, and I pitch forward, grabbing on to the edges of the nest. It's precarious at best, and I feel the branch beneath my feet bend.

"Miri!" I try again, desperate.

She stirs, opens her eyes.

Bolts upright.

"Don't. Move," I tell her, and something in my voice makes her listen immediately. "I'm right here, and I'll help you."

"Liv? What the hell is this?"

"Well, we are in a tree."

"A tree? What are you talking about?" Miri shifts toward me, and the entire tree sways.

"Stop!" I yell at her, shifting back fully onto a thicker branch, distributing my weight as evenly as I can and then grabbing for the tree's trunk instead of relying on the nest to hold me. "Miri, please listen."

But Miri is disoriented. She climbs to the edge of the nest.

"Liv, please. I'm so scared."

Our hands find each other in the dark, and I hold her tight as she climbs out of the nest.

"We'll go slow," I tell her.

"All right," she says.

We start our descent. Every inch is hard-earned in the dark, with our hearts about ready to break through our rib cages. I try not to focus on the ground so far below. Instead, I pay attention to the bark beneath my fingers. I tell Miri to dig her nails in, and we leave a trail of tiny crescent moons in the tree, marking our slow path downward. We stay close to each other, only allowing enough distance to step on different branches as we climb down.

We are nearing the end.

I can hear the others whispering below us, only too far to make out their words.

On Miri's next step, her foot lands on a branch that instantly cracks from her weight on it. I reach for her, but

I'm too slow, too far away, and I feel only a brush of air where she was a moment ago.

She doesn't even have time to scream.

There is only a small gasp of surprise, and she's gone.

The sound of her hitting the earth is dulled by the soft moss that grows all around, followed by Effie's shocked scream.

I hurry down the tree, swinging onto the lowest branch and letting myself drop. I lose my balance and slip, but I'm up a moment later, rushing to Miri's side.

She landed hard on one of the sprawling roots of the tree, right on her back.

I fall to my knees beside her.

"*Sweet Mother Mary,* that hurt," Miri whines through clenched teeth.

She's okay. Or at least okay enough to talk, and to complain.

She's already trying to stand, and we help her get up. I can already see the shadows forming along her spine—one massive bruise spreading from the nape of her neck down her back. It must hurt like hell, but Miri looks around, oblivious to it as she counts heads.

"Celia?" she asks.

"We're still looking for her," Rosa says.

"We have to find her," Miri says. She winces with every movement, but she doesn't complain again. Not with Celia unaccounted for.

"Miri, what happened? How did you get up there?" Effie

asks, putting her arm around her sister to support her as we start walking again.

"I have no goddamn idea," Miri answers.

We move away from the tree, fanning out into the forest. We stand farther apart to cover more ground, but still close enough to see each other. Miri and Effie stay together, and I know without asking that Miri is hurting worse than she's letting on by the way she walks, slightly hunched.

It isn't long before I hear Paris shout through the dark forest once again for us to stop. I wait in silence, trying to hear what Paris heard, but this time there's nothing.

"Over here," Paris calls out.

When we reach her, she is on her knees, leaning over with her ear pressed against the ground.

"What is it?" Rosa asks, and Paris waves her off, shushing her.

"She's here," Paris says.

"Where?" I ask, looking around.

Paris starts to dig furiously into the earth with her bare hands.

"What are you doing?" I ask. There is nothing in the dirt except a small hole—maybe large enough for a fox or a badger. "It's an animal den, Paris."

"She's under us," Paris says. "She's right beneath us. I can hear her."

She finally looks up to find the four of us staring at her.

"*Help me*," she demands.

We sink to our knees beside her and dig. I feel moss and soil and earthworms as they sift through my hands, grabbing everything I can reach by the fistful, over and over again until I'm mindless with it. I'm no longer questioning Paris, or what happened tonight.

Right now, my job is just . . . dig.

And then my fingers touch something smooth and soft. I pinch the fabric between my fingers. It's filthy, but familiar. A silk slip.

"Right here!" I shout, and the others crowd in closer to me, their fingers following the shape in the dirt beneath us.

We are archaeologists, but instead of unearthing an ancient burial site, we are exhuming a girl, praying for her resurrection. I find her shoulders, and we follow the gentle curve of them, trying to get her face out of the earth. We finally do, unveiling Celia, but she is covered in dirt, and her skin is cool to the touch.

"She isn't breathing," Effie says.

Rosa is shouting, brushing dirt away from Celia's eyes and nostrils.

Effie pulls Celia's mouth open, and we find it filled with more dirt. Paris moves back with a sharp cry of distress. I can hear her pacing behind me until she finally breaks and starts to cry, her soft sobs echoing through the woods.

"Roll her over," Effie says, shifting Celia to her side and using a finger to scoop dirt from between her lips.

"There," she says. "It's clear."

"C'mon, Celia. Breathe," I whisper.

"Breathe, goddamn it," Effie yells. She smacks Celia's back so hard that I wince at the sound.

"Again," Paris says from behind me. She is crouched, sitting on her haunches, like she can't decide whether to sit or stand. Tears quietly fall down her cheeks and onto her legs.

Effie strikes Celia's back again. A third time. It's an awful sound, a fist on flesh, and I want to cover my ears.

Then a gasp and a cough.

Celia rolls over, choking so hard she starts to throw up. It's more dirt than anything else. Paris crawls forward in the dirt, wrapping her arms tight around Celia, murmuring soft words of comfort that are only half intelligible.

For a while, the only sounds in the forest are their harsh breathing. Celia sucks in lungfuls of air for her oxygen-starved body, and Paris cries out in relief.

Beads of sweat roll down my face without stopping. I should be cold out here in the middle of the night, away from the bunker or the warmth of a fire. I feel the chill in the air around me and the cool of the moss beneath my bare feet, but it doesn't register as cold in my body. Instead, I feel overheated.

I reach for Miri's cool hand to comfort me, and I encounter more heat.

When I look at Miri, she is flushed, beads of sweat rolling off her body, too.

The hairs on my arms raise all at once. It's little more than a tickle of awareness, climbing up my spine like a paper-thin spider, resting on the nape of my neck, so real it's as if I could brush it away.

I feel the monster's eyes on me before I see her.

I turn slowly; I don't want to alarm the others. She's standing only a few yards away, in the shadow of a tree. If I took just a few steps, I could reach out and touch her.

The darkness clings to her like a shroud, and I can make out only the shape of her, her lithe form, her long kelplike hair, her arms that end in the wicked points of her nails. I see the shine of her eyes when the moonlight slips through the thick tree branches above, but I can't make out the features of her face.

I wait for her to attack. There is little we could do to defend ourselves. We ran out of the bunker with nothing. But she stays where she is. She slowly tilts her head like she did the night I followed her. Like she is listening closely. Studying us.

I force myself to look away from the creature. I keep my voice steady.

"We should probably go back now," I say to the others.

Rosa leads the way with the flashlight. Miri walks with Effie, their arms linked for support. Celia leans heavily on Paris.

I walk a few feet back from the others. If she does come for me, the sound will give the others some warning.

The mossy ground beneath me springs back after each slow step. I feel the wet sluice of mushrooms as they shred under my feet. My chest and cheeks are still flushed despite the chill, only now I can't blame it on the hot rush of exertion or fear.

I feel the spider on the back of my neck once more, and I know she's still behind me.

It takes every ounce of self-control I have to not turn around as we walk, to not do anything to alert the others. We can't panic. We can't run. She doesn't see us as prey right now, or as a threat, and we can't do anything to change that.

When we reach the bunker, I don't look until I'm turning to pull the door closed behind me.

She's right there. Her head is tilted, angled to the side as though her neck got twisted, but even as I watch, she straightens it and looks at me dead-on. I still can't make out her face, even this close.

"Liv," Effie calls up from below. She's standing at the foot of the steps. "Is everything all right? We need you down here."

"It's fine." My voice croaks out the words. My throat had gone dry as I stood there.

She followed us all the way here.

But she didn't hurt us.

She's more scared of you, Liv.

Everly's words spring up in my mind.

Dawn breaks in the sky above us as I pull the door shut tight. There's no option to lock it—the best I can do is make it flush with the wall, kicking loose dirt out of the way.

"What's wrong?" I ask when I reach the main room of the bunker.

Miri is lying on some of the cushions, with the others crowded around her, holding flashlights aimed at her. I lean over Paris to get a better look.

Miri's fists are clenching the soft blankets sprawled on either side of her. The bruises on her back have blossomed into brilliant shades of dark purple and green along the entire length of her body.

But it's her spine that brings me to my knees beside her.

The bones of her vertebrae have sharpened to points, and down the length of her back they are starting to break through her skin. There are small puncture wounds at each spot, with the barest hint of bone visible as it presses up and out of her body.

I scramble to find the first aid kit, reaching for the single remaining roll of gauze left tucked inside of it. With Effie's help, we wind the material around Miri's body, starting just above her breasts and working our way down. The fabric starts to turn crimson in all the places that it crosses her back, and when we finish there is a trail of red streaks down the center of the white material, outlining the curve of her spine. Highlighting every place where her skin has been torn open by protrusions of bone.

Effie finds one of the bottles of whiskey and pours it out one capful at a time, tipping it into Miri's mouth and encouraging her with soft murmurs to swallow it.

It's all we have to try to dull the pain.

Eventually there's nothing more we can do for her, but we all suffer alongside Miri just the same. Her soft whimpers keep us awake in the dark. Several times she cries out, her pain and terror echoing through the room, and I turn to her, murmuring nonsense words of comfort until she goes back to sleep. Or perhaps she loses consciousness.

I kiss her hot forehead. Her flushed cheeks. I can't help her pain, but I can make sure she knows she isn't alone.

We all finally give up on the notion of sleep. We lie in the dark, taking turns telling stories and singing songs. When Paris tries, her voice is only a husky imitation of its former strength. At one point we just cycle through the plots of our favorite television shows.

I have no idea how much time passes. We lie on the packed-earth floor of the bunker, all of us surrounding Miri, stretching out like petals from a flower's pistil.

Celia takes a turn at stories. She recalls what she can of *The Odyssey,* and Paris teases her for choosing yet another tale of a shipwreck. They've just washed across Circe's enchanted shores when Miri stirs.

"Water?" she asks in the dark, and we scatter from the floor in an instant to get her some. She takes a few sips and slips back out of consciousness.

It isn't until Odysseus is navigating Charybdis's vicious waters that Miri awakens again.

"I need to get out of the dark," she says.

"Of course," I tell her. "We'll help you."

I'm so relieved to hear her speak coherently, I could cry. I've missed the sound of her voice so much. When I take her hand, she squeezes mine, twice, a silent *Hello, I'm here. I'm with you.*

All of us stumble up the stairs of the bunker, so tired we feel drunk with it. When we emerge, it's already dusk. We've missed an entire day in the bunker, soothing Miri's pain.

Effie and Miri climb the bunker stairs last.

Miri blinks against the light, shielding her eyes. Effie leans her against the wall of the bunker and moves to her back to check her spine, assess the damage.

"Celia," Effie says. "Can you come here?"

Her voice is taut. It's a pitch I haven't heard before, and it sounds so strange coming from Effie that it takes me a moment to place the emotion that's so evident in her tone.

She's scared.

Celia joins them, helping Effie remove the wraps from around Miri to get a better look. Celia reaches for Miri but pulls back at the last second, as though she's afraid to touch her. Instead, she puts her hands on Miri's shoulders and helps her turn.

Miri's spine has erupted from her skin. The bones of her vertebrae twist together, creating a white braid of bone down her back.

And on either side of her spine, slowly unfurling in the sunlight, secured to that column of bone, are wings.

They are nothing like a bird's wings.

Miri's wings are gossamer silk—white and sheer at the same time. They remind me of moths. The most fragile kind, the ones with a whispered existence, that count their lives in hours, not days. The kind that turn to paper in your fingers, crumbling into nothing but dust at the slightest pressure.

Miri raises her arms, and the tendons exposed along her spine ripple in response, a cascading movement that shakes the wings loose, opening them fully. Beads of dew drip down the folds, following the network of veins that run through the radiant surface of them.

"Miri?" Effie asks softly, like she thinks her sister truly might take flight at the slightest provocation, disappearing into the atmosphere like ether. "Are you all right?"

Miri shivers, and the wings ripple in response. Part of her. "It's weird, but not . . . bad. Different. New."

We're still just animals, adapting to our environment. We evolve. Miri had said that to me when we slept together under the stars. My wounds change the structure of my skin and veins, twisting into something strange, but known. Terrible, but recognizable. But it is still part of me, made of my own flesh and blood.

I step closer to Miri. I can see that the wings aren't so much like a moth's at all. They look like nothing I've seen before—they are singularly Miri's. They don't look fragile, or like they're made of dust and scales. They look strong. There are tendons and veins fanning across their entire width.

Miri takes a few steps away from the bunker and spreads her arms.

The wings mirror the movement, stretching wide.

"Well, that's kind of wicked, actually," Miri says.

But Miri isn't the only one who got hurt last night.

I turn to Celia. "How are you feeling today? You weren't bleeding or bruised like the rest of us have been, but you were somehow buried alive, so . . ."

Celia opens her mouth, and I stop talking.

Her top and bottom incisors have grown into long, wicked points. She runs her tongue over them like she's learning the new shape of them.

"Fangs," she says. "I have bloody fangs. Like a vampire."

"It's some kind of infection, right?" Effie asks.

"Perhaps a toxin?" Celia poses. "Or some kind of metal? Something gets into our bloodstream when we get injured, or in my case, when our lungs have filled up with soil from the island. It might be a parasite."

"We're missing something," I say.

My arms, Miri's back, Celia's teeth. Rosa's foot and Paris's voice and ears and eyes. The only one unchanged is Effie.

Then I realize what else is different about us and Effie. I've grown so used to it that I stopped noticing it—the constant sticky sheen of sweat covering me. The flush of heat in my chest and cheeks at all hours of the day.

The others wear only the slips from the crate now, too. It's like we can't tolerate anything heavier touching our sensitive, too-hot skin.

Except Effie.

Effie is the only one standing there in layers. She has long pajama pants on, and my sweatshirt. Woolly gray socks that she swiped from Miri cover her feet.

"Effie, are you cold?" I ask.

"I'm freezing. We're somewhere in the northern Pacific Ocean. We're probably nearest Alaska, for god's sake. I don't know how the rest of you are hot."

"It's trauma," I whisper.

"What do you mean?" Celia asks.

"We've been thinking about it wrong. It isn't a toxin or a parasite or an illness, because it isn't hurting us. It only happens in places where we're injured. Our bodies are . . . healing. They're just healing differently from how they were before. My arm was horribly infected. You saw it, Celia. You dug *maggots* out of me. Did you think I would recover from that?"

Celia shakes her head. "I didn't. I thought for sure you'd develop sepsis. It was really bad."

"But I started to get better when I let *this* take over." I point to my arm where the wound once was, now stitched together in mushroom-shaped growths of skin and blood vessels. "It's not pretty, but it healed."

"This probably saved my foot from infection, too," Rosa points out, lifting her shining scaled foot. "It healed overnight."

"Paris lost her voice, but she gained superhuman hearing," I say. "We should all be cold right now, but we're not. Our bodies have adapted to the temperature."

"Celia, what do you think?" Paris asks, training her eerie blue eyes on the person she trusts most.

"I don't know," Celia says. "Honestly, it's completely bizarre. Living things don't usually adapt this fast, except on a microscopic level. We're talking about, like, *very* rapid evolution. But I think Liv is right. It's like an immune response. We transform as we heal."

"But that means there's nothing to stop the process, either," Rosa says. "Every time we get hurt, we'll change a little more."

"Until what?" Effie asks.

I have a guess as to the answer, but I don't want to say it out loud. If I'm wrong, there's no point. If I'm right, it's a terrifying thought.

In the end, I'm not the only one who draws the same conclusion.

"Her," Miri says. "We become like her."

We don't have to debate the merits of the argument this time.

The creature is womanlike but not human. Her nails and her hair. The way she's changed enough to live in water.

Maybe she's just not human *anymore.*

"If she was like us once, then maybe she doesn't want to hurt us. Maybe she's trying to tell us something. Warn us."

"Warn us that if we stay too long, we'll become the Creature from the Black Lagoon?" Paris asks.

"Basically, yes."

"Then why kill Vincent?"

"Maybe he went after her first," I say. "Or she perceived him as a threat. A predator."

"She wasn't entirely off base with that one," Miri says from where she's leaning against the bunker.

"You okay, Mir?" I ask. "You've obviously had the, um, biggest adjustment here."

"Are you kidding? I am a *literal* fairy. I have wings. Couldn't get any cuter if I were a goddamn bunny. This is my nightmare."

But then Miri turns in a graceful spin, unfurling her wings when she stops.

"Then again, they are quite pretty," she says. "I wonder if they work."

"We're *not* testing that theory," I counter.

Miri grins impishly. "Spoilsport."

"So what do we do now?" Paris asks. "Knowing the island is slowly morphing us into the Loch Ness monster doesn't change the fact that we're stranded here."

We fall quiet, unsure of what comes next. Understanding our transformations doesn't make the island any less terrifying, and it doesn't make us any less stuck here.

In the silence, there is a soft sound repeating over and over.

Scratch and hiss. Scratch and hiss.

It's Effie. She's holding Vincent's lighter in her hand, and she's flicking it open and shut, open and shut. I don't think she realizes she's doing it.

She's shrunk back away from the rest of us, and she looks suddenly small—smaller than I've ever seen her before. Not in stature, but in presence.

She's had surprisingly little to contribute to the conversation.

"Are you all right, Effie?" I ask.

"I'm so sorry," she whispers.

"It's not your fault, Ef. It was an accident that landed us here," Celia says. "We'll find a way."

"What if it wasn't?" Effie asks.

"Wasn't what?" Celia asks.

"An accident."

"Effie, what the hell are you talking about?" Miri asks.

"Vincent disabled the radios on purpose." Effie continues to flick the lighter. Open and shut. Open and shut.

"Explain better, and do it now," Celia says.

"He put a lot of money into the film. Too much. It was reckless. Impulsive. And then he was under all this pressure, and he needed it to do well or he'd lose everything."

"What did he do?" I ask.

"He wanted a few headlines. That's all. It was meant to look like a few days of us missing at sea. Long enough for some media coverage, and then he and Wilson were going to fix the communications for a miraculous rescue. Worthy of the front page of every newspaper. But Wilson . . ." Effie trails off. But we all know the rest.

Wilson jumped. And Vincent didn't know how to fix anything.

"Effie," Paris whispers. "How could you not tell us? All this time?"

Effie flicks the lighter again and Celia snaps, reaching out and knocking it from her hand into the dirt. "Enough!" Celia says.

"It's not her fault," Rosa says. "It was Vincent. She wasn't responsible for his actions."

"She could at least have told us the truth," I say.

"Well, that's rich, coming from you, *Everly*," Effie mumbles.

"Those aren't even *close* to the same thing," I say.

"What isn't?" Miri asks.

You're a liar, Liv Whitlock.

I can already hear the condemnation. I swore I'd be honest with her. I crossed my heart. And now right on the heels of her sister's lies, I have to admit mine, too.

I turn to Miri. "I'm sorry, I should have told you sooner."

"What the hell is it?" Miri asks.

"It wasn't my application."

"What?"

"It wasn't mine. It was my sister's information, all of it. Even her name."

"Why would you do that?" Miri asks. "What's your name?"

"It's Liv. Really. Liv is my name. It's short for Violet. Not Everly."

"Violet. And nothing I read about you in your file was real?" she clarifies. "You aren't class president, and you don't have perfect grades?"

"No. Definitely not. I have a juvenile record."

"You did all of that to win an internship, and *this* is where you end up?" Miri says, and then she laughs. "Wow, you might have the worst luck of all of us."

"Wait . . . you aren't mad at me? For lying?"

"Liv, I don't want you to lie to me about important things.

I don't give a fly's tit what grades you had or what your full legal name is on a piece of paper. Besides, I already knew you were a liar. That's why I tell you that you are one all the time.

"And as for you." Miri whirls on her sister. Effie might be the elder sister and stand six inches taller, but in this moment, it's clear that Miri has the authority. "You will stop blaming yourself for Vincent's crimes, starting right now."

"Mir, you don't have to—"

"Yes, we do. We have to get it through your thick skull. Vincent was an awful, evil man. He manipulated you. He *hurt* you, Effie, when you were still a child. So screw him, and all of his stupid plans to make headlines by faking a maritime disaster, only to actually cause a maritime disaster. I mean, the man was an idiot, Ef. And we've let him take up enough of our lives."

"So . . . you aren't mad?"

"I'm furious, Effie. But I forgive you."

Celia steps forward, a serious look on her face. "Wait, Effie, you said he turned off the radios on purpose?"

"Yeah, why?"

"I might be able to use it," Celia says. "I mean, it's a long shot, especially after this long underwater, but the emergency systems should have held up for at least . . ."

"Are you saying you might be able to call for help?" I ask.

"I mean, the emergency phone is still our best bet, but

with our luck, it's drifted to Russia by now. But we can try. If they just disabled the radios, then maybe we can salvage them."

There is a wild thrumming in my veins. It's as strange as the shape of my fingers. It's as foreign and forgotten as the sensation of cold. It's a feeling I've had little experience with my whole life: hope.

This might work. We could leave this island and its strangeness behind us forever.

We could go home.

ACT IV

The Point of No Return

Shake it off.

—*The Tempest,* Act I, Scene II

26

Nine Months Later

I wait until I'm right behind her to unsheathe my knife.

I've sharpened the blade against stone in the creek, and I know how easily it will cut through skin and the tender arteries of a throat. I'm counting on it.

There is still an echo of guilt inside of me, reminding me that I don't really want to do this. But my hunger is louder. As always in this place, it is the one that wins.

One swift, sure pull of the blade against flesh, and it's done.

Hot blood spills onto my hands.

I drop the body onto the ground and watch as the earth around her turns crimson, then black. It's always a surprise to me just how much blood there is.

"It's done," I call back to the woods.

Rosa and Paris emerge from the shadowed coverage of the trees.

"Thank you," Rosa says. "I just couldn't do it."

"It's fine," I tell her. I could add something else. I could say I'm used to it, but I'm not. I could say we're only doing what is necessary, but she already knows that.

"She's beautiful," Paris says, her voice the familiar soft rasp we're now used to. She gives our kill a wide berth as the blood soaks into the ground. Paris is barefoot, as we all are. My sneakers finally gave out during the winter, falling to pieces as I ran through the mossy wet forest during a storm. But our feet have grown callused, and it doesn't really hurt anymore.

"We're going to win," Rosa says, and there's a chirp of genuine giddiness in her voice.

"Of course we're going to win," I say. "We've been the better hunters from the start."

I kneel on the ground, my knees sinking into blood-soaked soil. I place my knife at the navel and cut a straight line up. The intestines are easy to remove, and I scoop them carefully into the sack on my hip.

Volatile and occasionally violent, they called me. A condemnation.

But that violence serves me well in this place.

"Should we drag the body back?" Rosa asks, her tone casual as she considers our options.

"We could butcher her out here, but it's almost dusk," I say, checking the sun's position in the sky. "And we're strong enough to take her. She's small. We can pull her."

Our bodies have changed in a hundred ways.

Paris's pale pink hair grew out, leaving her natural light brown in its place. Paired with the shocking blue of her transformed eyes, Paris is striking, even before you notice the strangeness of her wide, thin ears.

We are stronger. No longer starving. Paris has muscles rippling beneath her thighs and calves as she bends to help lift the body. So do I. And Rosa was always strong, except those first few weeks, when we were still so hungry. When we hadn't figured out what we needed to do to survive here.

The netting that caught our prey is still wrapped around the legs. I gently untangle it, careful not to break the net. We'll need it again.

We are able to lift the body between two of us, rotating the third person out for a rest when it gets too heavy. We stop at the tallest tree in the forest on our way. I untie the canvas sack from my hip, where it was dripping a steady stream of blood and bile down my leg. I hang it on a low branch of the tree, where it's easily found.

She'll know to look there.

We always leave an offering after a kill.

In return, she'll leave us something, too. Maybe a skull. Maybe a rib. They aren't particularly useful, but we collect each item with reverence, lining the walls of our home with her gifts.

We make good time back to the bunker, and I can hear voices before we crest the last hill.

One voice rings out above the others, directed right at me.

"Oi! You little brats! Don't tell me you got another doe!" Miri yells from below.

"Fine!" I call back. "I won't tell you."

We drag the deer down the ridge and into the clearing outside the bunker.

Miri, Effie, and Celia stand before us, looking properly ready for battle. Miri's filthy, covered head to toe in blue dust. Her wings peek out from behind her back, and they're shimmering blue, too.

It's from the lichen that cover the trees on the eastern side of the island, the cliff side.

"Were you in the trees again?" I ask.

"Naturally," Miri quips.

I already know what she's got behind her back.

"Please don't tell me it's another—"

"It's a bald eagle!" Miri shouts, bringing her bounty from behind her and setting it in between us, next to our deer.

"Not another one," Paris groans.

"We asked you not to," Rosa says.

"It's not *our* beloved national bird," Effie says, shrugging.

"What is our national bird, anyway?" Miri asks.

"I don't think that's something people care to know—outside of America, that is," Effie intones.

"It's the robin, actually," Celia says.

"Isn't this, like, cannibalism for you, Miri?" I gesture to the dead eagle at my feet and then her.

"I'm not a *bird*," Miri says with mock offense. "Why are you lot so sentimental about the eagles, anyway?"

"Well, we're not, really. It just feels wrong," Rosa says.

"I think they're endangered," Paris adds.

"Well, so are we," Celia says. "I'm eating the bird." She moves to our firepit, which we've lined with stone on all sides to help trap the heat longer, and make our fires burn hotter.

"We still win," I say.

"Yeah, all right, take your tally, then," Effie says. She walks over to the door of the bunker and lifts the nail we keep hanging by a ribbon for just this occasion. Carved into the door are two words. *Brits* on one side. *Yanks* on the other. Effie carves a mark below *Yanks*.

"Fifteen to nine," I read, tsking my disappointment. "You three really need to start pulling your weight around here. You're giving an entire kingdom a bad name."

"Our kingdom already had a bad name, thank you," Celia lectures from where she's pulling feathers off the eagle. "Imperialism, colonialism . . . you're not the only nation celebrating independence from us every year, right? Not by a long shot."

Once the meat is sizzling over the flames, we gather at our stone table. Rosa passes around a basket woven from the reeds that grow at the creek, filled with greens and a few handfuls of the wild carrots and strawberries that we'd found growing in the spring.

After our meal, Miri sprawls in the dirt, wings folded

haphazardly under her. They've held up remarkably well considering how careless Miri is about them.

She shifts across the ground until her head is in my lap like a pillow.

"Liv," she drawls. It's the tone she uses when she wants something.

"Yes?" I ask.

"Do you remember last year, when you promised you would never, *ever* lie to me, and then we learned you'd actually lied to me about everything, even your name?"

"I remember, Miri."

"And do you remember how divinely generous I was to forgive you essentially right away?"

"Yes, Miri. I remember."

"Exactly. I knew you'd see my side," she says.

"Your side of what?" I ask.

"My imperfect side," she explains. "The one that decided to take these babies for a little—very minor and completely safe—spin earlier today."

My brain takes a moment to process it all.

"You flew?" I am truly stunned. She'd joked about it so many times, I'd stopped taking her threats seriously.

"Well, I fell first. About seven—"

"Eight!" Celia calls from the far end of our table.

"—eight times."

"And the ninth time?"

"She flew," Effie says. "Only for a minute, only gliding, and she crash-landed in a prickle bush. But she did it."

"You aren't supposed to encourage her," I scold Effie.

"She's your girlfriend," Effie says. "Talk some sense into her before she breaks her neck."

When the moon is high above us, we put out the fire and file down to our bunker. We pass around a jar and take turns scooping out a bit of waxy honeycomb onto our fingers that we put in our ears.

It took us ages to figure it out. We couldn't see how all the events were connected until one night mid-spring. It was Celia's week to tell stories, and she was retelling *The Odyssey* for the third or fourth time. Odysseus had just traveled past the sirens when I shot straight up on my mattress.

"Oh my god, the sirens," I said to the dark room of the bunker. "She's like the sirens."

"What are you talking about?" Miri asked sleepily from behind me.

"That last night on the *Bianca,* Vincent heard singing. He distinctly said he heard a voice—do you remember that? He got mad at us when we didn't hear it, too."

"It was the wind," Effie said.

"What if it wasn't? What if he heard *her*? And Wilson, too. Remember what he said before he jumped?"

"He said, 'It's so beautiful,'" Effie recalled.

"He *heard* her. Like the sirens. Vincent heard it again, our first night on the island. He followed it into the woods. And I think . . . I think we've been following it, too."

"But we've never heard voices, Liv."

"No, but we sleepwalk. Across the island. Into eagle nests on top of trees. Celia, you buried yourself alive."

There were more incidents, too. We found Effie walking into the ocean to drown herself. We found Celia hunting in the night, with a squirming rabbit caught in her bloodied mouth. I woke kneeling at the creature's pool, time and time again, staring at my faceless reflection in her mirrored waters.

"What if it's calling us," I wondered. "Compelling us. What if we hear it in our sleep without even knowing it?"

The others weren't convinced, so the next day, I gathered the honeycomb for the first time.

None of us had sleepwalked since.

The others think that we realized too late what is wrong with the island. I disagree. I think we realized it too soon. We realized it before the sweet oblivion of our monstrosity could pull us down into that fever dream forever.

We continue to change, piece by piece. Every injury is graced by a transformation. Celia's fingernails become claws. Rosa's hair twists into kelp. Some of us became ill over winter, and when the coughs finally abated, our voices went with them, replaced by the same strange, low growl that Paris had.

The island is like a mouth, slowly consuming us. It is both the hunger and the ache, digesting the parts of us it finds most tender.

Making us just like her.

Effie is the last of us to change. She disappears in the night, like Miri and Celia did so many months ago, but we don't realize she's gone until morning.

We search the island for hours. Paris listens closely for any indication of where Effie went, but only shakes her head in each new place we check for her.

There is nothing. No sign of her at all.

"The grove," I say finally, driven by desperation more than hope after so many futile hours spent in pursuit of her.

We've carved out paths around the monster's blue lair. She doesn't attack us, but she likes to watch us. Sometimes she comes to the crest overlooking our bunker, head tilted, observing us from above. We try not to dwell on it. She doesn't harm us. But it's still unnerving every time we notice her, and we avoid her pool in the woods the best we can.

We break our rules in search of Effie.

When we reach the grove, my stomach churns with an

awful instinct. I climb down first, slowly, watching the water for any sign of movement. Just because the creature hasn't killed us yet doesn't mean she won't.

I peer into the water. At first, I see only my own face in the reflection. I've just cleaned my hair in the creek. Rosa pulled it into tight braids for me before our hunt.

My left eye is my natural brown, but my right eye is now clear blue, just like Paris's, from when I lost a battle with a wildcat and ended up with a scratched cornea. My arms have ribbons of lichen and mushrooms growing from my flesh—marking every single place I've injured it.

My eyes finally adjust, focusing beyond my reflection and into the pool itself.

In the moment it takes me to recognize her, I think it's the creature, rising from the depths of her pool to pull me under.

But I'm wrong.

It's Effie. She's floating just beneath the surface of the water, eyes closed like she's asleep. Her lips are parted, showing just a glimpse of her teeth. A tendril of small air bubbles still clings to the edge of her mouth, unmoving.

There is something on her neck, long and black and curving. It takes me a moment to realize it's her. The creature is right there beneath Effie, claws wrapped around Effie's throat.

And then the claws dig into Effie's flesh, and tear at her throat.

At the same moment I reach for her, Effie's eyes open wide, and she screams, a stream of bubbles underwater.

She bursts from the water, gasping for air.

"Effie." I grab for her, pulling her out of the water and onto the edge of the pool beside me. The others have caught up, crowding around her on every side.

We wait for the creature to follow, but she never does.

We hold Effie like that for a long time, hands pressed against her throat to stop the bleeding. Only now that she's out of the water, I can see that the creature didn't dig her claws deep into Effie's throat. It's merely a flesh wound.

When Effie's breathing slows, steadies, I pull back the sodden ropes of her hair so I can get a better look at the wound, noticing how hot Effie's skin is against my palm.

That's when I see it. Behind her ear, and just underneath it. Effie has already changed.

She has gills.

Effie swears it was an accident.

She forgot the honeycomb, and the siren must have called her, and she sleepwalked right into that crystalline pool in the woods, ready to drown herself under the creature's enchantment.

Except we always check for the honeycomb at night. We remind each other, and always check the ears of the girls sleeping nearest us.

We're so careful.

The other option is that Effie didn't use it on purpose, knowing the creature might sing her to her death.

That's the possibility that haunts us. We take turns keeping watch overnight, terrified that Effie will do it again. Miri and I whisper in the dark after the others are long asleep.

"She never let it go," Miri says on the third night after Effie's incident. "She blames herself."

"I know she does," I tell her.

"She will as long as we're here," Miri says. "The guilt is going to kill her."

"We won't let it," I whisper.

"Swear it," she says.

I pull Miri's arm to me in the dark and place her hand on my chest.

"Cross my heart," I promise.

I hold Miri's hand in the dark and squeeze it, twice. *I'm here with you*. I tell her we aren't done discussing it. I tell her that we'll find a way to get Effie to forgive herself, to find a home here with us.

Because I know what Miri is most scared of. Not that we won't ever find a way home, but that we'll never find a way to keep Effie safe, not from the creature or the island, but from herself.

I think that must be what drives Miri to the cliff.

I'm still half asleep when I turn to wrap my arms around Miri in the dark.

We'd stayed awake together long into the night talking about Effie. I know Miri had the honeycomb in when she fell asleep. I checked three times, tucking her blond hair behind her ears and letting the soft curls of it twist and tangle on my fingers.

But when I wake, my arms are empty.

Fear hollows out every bone in my body. I am untethered, like I'm floating up above myself, looking down at the place where Miri should be sleeping.

We go to the grove first, but it is empty except for the creature asleep in her lair. We start again the way we did when we were looking for Effie, crossing the island systematically, checking all the places that we've found each other in the past.

"She could have fallen," Celia says.

It's a fear that followed us for months before we started using the honeycomb. We worried that one of us would sleepwalk right off the eastern edge of the island and fall and break on the rocks below.

The sky is gray-pink as we make our way to the cliffs, quiet, contemplative. It's nearly sunrise now.

And then I see her.

Miri is standing on the very edge of the cliffs, facing the sea. Her strange, translucent wings are outstretched, and the first streaks of pink morning light catch on them, so they look almost illuminated.

She turns back at the sound of us emerging from the woods.

Miri isn't sleepwalking. She isn't responding to the creature's call, but fully awake and aware. She is standing so close to the edge that I cannot breathe.

She smiles at me. Her face is calm; only her eyes are slightly swollen from getting such little sleep. From so many hours in the dark, worrying about Effie.

The sun breaks on the horizon behind her, surrounding her in the warmth of a golden glow. *It is the east, and she is the sun.*

Instead of coming to us, she edges forward, until her toes hang over the edge. The second it takes me to understand Miri's intention is a second that costs me dearly. As soon as I surge forward to grab her, Miri jumps.

A cry is wrenched from somewhere deep inside of me

when I reach the ledge, and it is empty. I stand in the place where Miri stood half a second ago, and I can only watch in horror as her small form plummets toward the rocks.

At the very last moment, her arms spread. Miri's wings open, catching the wind.

She rises.

Miri streaks past us, lifting higher and higher, turning and circling as she goes, until she is just barely there, a small speck in the clouds. A girl who is no longer a girl, but something different. She's transformed into something else, something ancient and otherworldly. A creature of folklore and legend. We can't keep pretending we are the same lost girls who wrecked here. We have evolved into something new, changed forever by our traumas.

And then I hear it on the wind.

A strange, low keening. It is a mournful sound, and I realize that I've heard it before. On the *Bianca*, a thousand years ago, the night we wrecked. I heard it again on the shore one night in our first few weeks on the island, when she took me with her and saved my life.

The siren's song is one of mourning. She is the Greek chorus, trying to warn us away from this place. Instead, the beauty of her song calls us to her, an unintentional lure.

I hear her clearly now, and for the first time, I understand her.

High above us, the heavens shift.

A violent crosswind tears across Miri's body, and the angle is wrong.

We can do nothing but watch as the wind rips one of Miri's wings clean off her body, sending her plummeting back to the earth.

I am stuck in an awestruck horror as I watch her fall. I wonder if it is predestined. Some kind of fated divination, like the ancient poets wrote about. Icarus flew. Icarus fell. Every iteration of his story ends in tragedy. I can't help but think the same is true of all of us. Miri flew. Miri fell.

This was always going to happen.

She was dead from the beginning.

I expect the sound of a body breaking to be awful. It should be loud and cracking and violent, but Miri hits the ground with a soft *thump*.

She lands on a pile of raised earth and pine needles and moss, eyes closed. I've watched her sleep countless times, and she looks no different now.

Her cheeks are like rosebuds, wind-bitten but flushed with the promise of blood and life. I can smell the sweet-sour death notes in the area around her. And though the warmth hasn't quite left her face, the tips of her fingers are already a bright cerulean blue.

It is the color that flickers at the edge of a flame, or the flash of a fish scale in water. It is the color of the aurora borealis when it breaches the northern skies, dancing above a frigid ocean, an island lost to time, the intertwined bodies of two girls on a mountaintop.

It is also the color of death.

The skin of her shoulders is too pale. Her bloodlessness is a stark contrast to the bottle-green moss all around her. She is sprawled on a raised mound of pine needles and earth, and a trail of small indigo mushrooms encircles her head like a crown.

Sunlight slips through the thick forest canopy from above where all the branches are broken from trying to catch a falling star. The light illuminates the scene below like a spotlight on a stage.

From a distance, the soft dusting of blade-shaped scales above her ears could be mistaken for white-blond hair, and the protrusions from her back are hidden beneath the strange stillness of her body.

Strange, so long as I cling to the hope she is merely sleeping. Not so strange if I accept that she's dead.

Her remaining wing is bent beneath her.

A single drop of blood perches on the edge of her lips, and I watch as it slips, running from the corner of her mouth to the hollow beneath her ear, leaving a crimson trail in its wake.

Swear it, I imagine Miri saying to me now. *Swear you'll keep Effie safe.*

"Cross my heart," I whisper aloud. I make the promise I know she'd want, even though she can no longer demand it.

The others kneel around her, knees pressed against knees to form a semicircle. A crescent moon around Miri's small, broken body. The sun hasn't penetrated the trees yet, and we are all cast in the eerie gray-yellow of mornings on our island.

I realize that the island isn't waking up around us. There are no birds singing. No rabbits stirring in the brush around us. I know before I look up that she's there, watching us.

The creature steps into the clearing, approaching us quickly. The others back away, but I lift Miri into my arms, her lifelessness so heavy as she hangs limp in my embrace.

When the creature is near us, she stops. She waits. I'm not sure why I do it—why I trust her in this moment, out of all the time we've spent here on the island. I stand, barely able to hold Miri in my arms with her wing dangling unnaturally beneath her.

The creature only stands there, patiently, ready to relieve me of my burden.

I let the siren take Miri's body.

When she turns back for the woods, we follow.

I'm not paying attention to where we walk until the blue hazy glow of the creature's grove envelops us both.

She's brought Miri to her home.

The others wait at the top, letting me follow the creature and Miri down the embankment alone.

When the creature steps right into the pond with Miri, I don't hesitate to follow them.

The water ripples all around me before settling as flat as glass. I lean forward, studying my face. Liv in the reflection reaches up. She pulls at the side of her face, and I watch as it smears like paint on a canvas, trailing the colors of my skin and hair and one blue eye along with it.

Hands rise out of the pool all around me, mirrored below, so I can't see what they belong to. They wrap around my legs, reach for the hem of my slip, pulling me down. Nails sink into the flesh of my thighs, relentless.

The water slips over my head, and still the hands tug me down, down to the depths of the creature's pool. I try to find Miri in it, but she's gone.

My lungs ache in my chest. I start to fight in earnest, tearing the hands off me, but for every single one I free, several more take its place, holding me there.

The siren is in front of me, and she places her hand against my forehead. Her touch is gentle on my skin, and I hear her low, mournful song.

A thousand images filter through my mind, so fast I catch only the impressions of them.

There is a girl, barely older than us, with waves of black hair down her back. Her hands are bound, and her white Victorian nightgown is torn. She has streaks of blood on the insides of her thighs. She is limp as a rag doll when they throw her off the ship. But she washes ashore, on an island I recognize.

When she wakes, she feasts on blue fruit and drinks from a crystalline pool deep in the forest. When she's hurt, the island heals her, making itself part of her, piece by piece. When men come to her island, she lets it consume their bodies, or she kills them herself.

And when she's lonely, she sings, the sound altered by her elongated vocal cords to a pitch that no longer sounds human. Instead, it sounds like the wind on the sea. It calls others to her, even when she doesn't mean to.

I see soldiers encroaching on her island. They dig up the earth and kill the trees. They steal her food, her water, her home. She kills them, too.

Then one night, she finds something unexpected on the shore.

She finds girls. Girls like the one she once was.

I can feel the tingle of her shock at seeing us on her island, plus an emotion so human—and now so foreign to her ancient body—that it takes her a long time to even recognize it.

She is curious.

She slinks into the ocean to explore our wreck. She pulls us from the depths of the water, where some of us were drowning. She drags us onto the shore.

And then she hovers just out of sight, watching us, day after day after day.

Through her eyes, I see myself, standing in the ocean at night, basking in the moonlight and the sound of water crashing on rock. She knows that I am dying. She can smell the poison of infection in my blood.

She brings me here, to her most sacred place, and she shows me how the island will heal me, if I would only let it.

Through her eyes, I see Effie. I watch her rise from the bunker and walk through the woods, pulling the honeycomb out as she walks and dropping it into the leaves. I watch as Effie ties stones to her feet and puts more in the pockets of the dress she slept in, which I now realize was just for the purpose of filling her pockets with enough weight to drown her.

I see Effie again, underwater, eyes wide. Drowning, until the creature claws gills into the side of her neck.

Now I am lifting Miri's body from my own arms. I am carrying her body here, and sinking underwater with her. I wrap Miri's remaining wing around her, cocooning her in like a moth.

I reach out, placing my long fingers against my own forehead. One last attempt to tell my story, even as I'm dying. Even as I give my life for the winged girl.

Suddenly, I am back in my own body again. The creature is gone, and Miri is writhing in the water, struggling to break free from the skintight hold she is in.

I untangle her from her wing, and it tears off her in waterlogged pieces that sink to the bottom of the pool. I push Miri up, and she breaks through the surface and sucks in lungful after lungful of air. The others help us climb from the water.

She isn't dead. Miri isn't dead.

That's when I notice the creature. She's lying on the ground beside the water, unmoving.

I step over to her, gently pulling her hair back so I can see her face. She somehow looks both young and ancient. Her skin is sallow, cheeks sunken. A flush of scales crosses her cheek. Perhaps she is more creature than girl now, after all this time on the island, adapting to it. Evolving with it. But she is also still a girl. A girl who gave her life for Miri.

There is a memory just at the edge of my consciousness. One of the flashing scenes that she showed me. They went so fast, leaving only fleeting images behind, but there is one that snagged in my mind like a blanket caught on a branch.

I can see letters on the edge, right along a jagged piece of metal. *B-I-A*. There is something gleaming in the darkness—fluorescent green against gray shadows.

It's the emergency phone's box. Sunk with the front half of the ship, so deep in the ocean that Rosa never would have seen it. A depth that none of us could have held our breath long enough to reach even if we'd known it was there.

But that was before the island changed us.

One Year Later

Effie Knight's pitch-black eyes stare up at me.

For a second, I'm back at the edge of that blue water, discovering her half-drowned body all over again. Then my gaze refocuses on the magazine cover in front of me, and I find the lemon-yellow words printed below her face: *Effie Knight, Cult Leader? Plus! The Lipstick She Can't Get Enough Of.* I smile at the absurdity of it and slide that magazine over, scanning the next one. *The True Story of the NoPa 6: Turn to Page 47 for the Dark Details of the* Bianca's *Final Days.*

I pick up the entire stack of magazines and carry them to the door, dropping them into the garbage can. Only nice stories get to stay on the shelves.

There is a man yelling somewhere in the store behind me, but he's silenced by one glare. My mismatched eyes tend to make people uncomfortable. And that's before they even notice my arms.

I meet Miri in the parking lot, climbing into her car.

"Provisions?" she asks. When I don't answer right away, she waves her hand in front of me. "Hello in there!"

"Sorry!" I snap out of it and see the concern on her face. "It's nothing. Just more stupid magazines. They've nicknamed us the 'NoPa Six.'"

"What's that mean?"

"It stands for Northern Pacific. They're saying no one can find the island again. They went back using the coordinates from our rescue, but they're off somehow. So I guess 'Northern Pacific' is as specific as they can get. Not that they believe there even *was* an island. Apparently, we run a cult."

Miri crinkles her nose in distaste.

"They'll lose interest eventually," she reminds me. It isn't the first time we've had this conversation. "They're grasping at nothing since none of us will grant a single interview."

She's right, and I tell her so.

Miri drives us home. It's not a far drive from the small English village that her grandparents grew up in. She's bought a cottage on the coast, and we spent all morning decorating it for our anniversary before running out to the shop. There are bright blue streamers strung in the doorways and bowls of every kind of junk food we can imagine.

Miri tears open a bag of chocolate chips to snack on while we finish decorating.

Sweets are her latest favorite indulgence, and we've made it a practice to never deny ourselves our simple desires. We don't limit our hot showers, standing in the steam until our fingers and toes prune, sometimes worse than they did the morning of our shipwreck. We burn the fancy candles right away. We pop the expensive champagnes sent by her managers, agents, famous actors and actresses, drinking them lazily or all at once, depending on whatever mood strikes us.

We no longer ask for permission. We don't ask for forgiveness, either. We don't save anything for some imagined future occasion. Instead, we act as though every day is the one we've been waiting for. We learn to live fully in the present.

When we first got back, we tried to slip back into the lives we'd left behind, and for a while we pretended that it was possible. I went back to California. I tried to reconnect with my sister, to find a path forward together. But it was all wrong. I felt so out of place, I wanted to claw my skin off to escape it, because it wasn't my home. It never really had been.

The island had felt like more of a home, and at some point in all of our time there, the girls I'd been lost with had become my family. So, when Miri invited me to move in with her, I was on a plane that same day.

Even together, we struggled to adjust. Sometimes at night the walls of the cottage felt like they were closing in on us. It became so unbearable that Miri and I began sleeping on the beach in a pile of blankets, until one evening I arrived home to find Miri on the roof with a sledgehammer, slamming through the shingles, letting pieces of wood and debris rain down into the bedroom below.

"Oi!" I yelled up to her. "Don't tell me you broke the house again!"

"All right," Miri called down. "I won't tell you."

It rained the next two days. The tarp that Miri assured me would hold slipped off the roof not once, but twice, pouring cold rain into the room where we slept.

She finally agreed to let me hire someone to install the glass. After that, Miri and I would fall asleep with our heads pressed together, watching the stars and imagining we were somewhere else. We always sleep with the windows open now, even during storms. I drift off every night to the sounds of Miri breathing and the ocean waves rocking against the shore. My fingertips find the long scars on her spine, and I wonder if she dreams of flying.

One night, I mention to her in passing that I think I'd like to try writing again, and on my birthday, she fills an entire bookcase with blank notebooks for me to fill. When I do finally get brave enough to try it, I press the pages into her hands and ask her to read them for me.

Miri reads my poems aloud. She performs them. She does it standing on our bed, and on our kitchen table. Once from the top of the same roof she battered in. For Miri Knight, all the world is a stage, and it always will be. We keep trying to leave the island behind, but it is impossible to do so completely. Its wildness clings to us. Sometimes I miss the feel of a knife in my hand or the sensation of the creature's eyes watching me from the darkest part of the forest. She became as familiar as blood and fever and the sprouts of blue mushroom erupting from my fingertips.

It's strange to long for a place that tried so earnestly to kill you. But eventually, something shifts. I think of the island less and lean in to my new life more.

The others arrive in the afternoon, just as black summer storm clouds roll in off the sea. We are laughing over a bottle of wine when the thunder cracks overhead. At one point, lightning strikes the sand just outside our front door.

"That would be bloody terrifying," Celia says. "If we hadn't already survived a massive shipwreck and being stranded on an island."

"Speaking of it: a toast to our rescue. Exactly one year ago today." I lift my glass, and the others join me, recalling the day that we were found.

Effie tucks her hair back, and I note the curved slits behind her ear, typically hidden from view, but here, with us, she doesn't care.

It took her three dives to reach the emergency satellite phone. She was so exhausted I thought she'd collapse, but she wouldn't give up. She couldn't. She *had* to save us.

When she finally found the box, she said it was exactly

where I described it would be, tucked into the broken bow of the ship where it came to rest deep in the ocean offshore.

When Celia first turned the satellite phone on, nothing happened. And then a steady, blinking red light appeared on the side.

Three days later, a rescue team arrived.

One year ago today, we left the island.

"I'm just relieved you've finally put the roof back on," Rosa says, pointing up at the skylight and calling me back from my reverie.

Paris sits down and Celia immediately reaches for her, pulling her in to sit closer and weaving their arms together so their skin touches in every place it can. Paris wears her hair down in public, letting it cover the strange shape of her ears, and Celia learns to smile with her upper lip covering her sharpened teeth. Rosa has a different response to her changes. She starts swimming competitively. When asked by a reporter if her changed body gave her an advantage over others, Rosa replied, "I hope so. I have room at home for more gold medals."

Miri and I simply retreat, content to live in our own little bubble away from prying eyes, at least for now. I imagine one day the stage will call her name again, and I'll be there to watch her from the front row.

We eat our dinner the way we did on the island, sitting crisscross on the floor at a low table. None of us can tolerate chairs yet. We eat with our fingers, not bothering to put up a polite front in the privacy of our home. Here we can be every bit as feral as we were out there, and we often are. I pile my plate with pasta and fruit and cheese.

We've all given up meat.

It doesn't taste right if we didn't kill it ourselves.

"Why do you think she did it?" Effie asks later. "Why did she die for us?"

We finished our meal and are sitting on the beach together. The sand is still wet from the rain, but we hardly even notice it. None of us is bothered by the cold, even now.

I'm staring at the line where the sky meets the sea. It's a line I stared at for so many months.

Effie's question is one we've asked before. Back on the island, waiting for rescue those last few days. It's a question without an answer, except for what I saw in the creature's memories. The pieces we could put together.

"Because she was like us," I say. "Just a girl. At least she used to be, before she became a monster."

"She wasn't ever really a monster, though, was she?" Miri says. "She was Ariel. The spirit of the island. Enchanted and trapped by the villain Sycorax."

"Until we freed her," I say. I rub the tips of my fingers together, over the ridges and valleys of skin, so similar to the clusters of blue mushrooms on our island that it always makes me feel like I'm there, running my hands over the bark of a tree until I find the peculiar indigo growths along the side. We've tried to find the name of them, but it's been a hopeless endeavor. I wonder if they only grow there, born of something particular to that place.

Like us.

"Do you think people can change?" Rosa asks, stretching her legs out in the sand and letting her scales catch the sliver of moonlight peeking out of the clouds.

"That's not the right question," I say, smiling at a memory.

"Then what is?" Rosa asks.

"The right question is," Miri says, leaning forward with the ghost of a smile on her lips, "can people stay the same?"

Her hand finds mine, squeezing it tight, even though I'm never afraid of the dark when Miri is near. It was never the darkness I feared, but the promise it made, that I was all alone in this world. Now I never feel that loneliness. The six of us will always be together on that island, no matter where we go. We keep adapting to our environment, even now.

We can't help it.

We evolve.

Acknowledgments

My first acknowledgment is to you, reader. Writing and publishing books is an incredible honor, and it's not one that I take for granted. I wouldn't be able to send a message in a bottle without someone waiting to fish it out of the water. So, first and foremost, thank you for reading. I wrote this book for you.

Bad Graces might be the most twisted idea I've had yet, so I'm both surprised and very glad that I got the chance to write it. I'm even more grateful that people are now finding their way to this strange island and its lost girls. When I began writing this book, I knew it was about trauma—how we heal from it, how it changes us, and why that change is okay and often necessary. It wasn't until a later draft that I realized *Bad Graces* is also very much about loneliness and forging connections even in the harshest of conditions, when hope is most fragile. I think sometimes loneliness can feel exactly like being stranded on an island. I've stood on those shores. But just like the NoPa 6, we keep our eyes on the horizon, because that's what ships are made for.

I am so fortunate to continue working with my wonderful editor, Ben Rosenthal. This is the fourth book I've had the privilege of working on together. Thank you for embracing this story for exactly what it was, and then making sure that it became the best version of itself before we sent it out into the world. Thank you as well to the incredible publishing team who contributed to *Bad Graces*, including Patty Rosati, Mimi Rankin, Josie Dallam, Christina Carpino, Joel Tippie, James Neel, Kristen Eckhardt, Mikayla Lawrence, Gwen Morton, Lisa Calcasola, and Kelly Haberstroh. Thank you, Katya Murysina, for creating some truly gorgeous art for the cover of *Bad Graces*.

I'm so thankful for my agent, Suzie Townsend, who is a steadfast advocate for my work and simply unmatched in dissuading my fears. Thank you for answering a million questions (and counting) and for never doubting we would find a home for my words. Thank you to Sophia Ramos and the dedicated and talented team at New Leaf Literary.

I'm endlessly grateful to my family for their support of my writing. Thank you to my beautiful mom, who keeps buying so many copies of my books to give away, even when I insist that I have extra copies for her. Thank you to my aunts and uncles, who are so wonderfully quick to buy my books on the day they come out and spread the word far and wide to friends. I'm certain that an impressive percentage of my book sales can be traced directly back to you.

Thank you to Kayleigh and Katharyn for talking to me through panicked phone calls when I thought I'd run out of words. You were right: I had more. And thank you, forever, to Andrew, Rowan, and Theo, for being the absolute greatest cheerleaders of dreams I could ask for. I love you to every corner of the multiverse and back.